Dirt

K F Ridley

LRP

DIRT

Copyright 2012 KF Ridley

www.kfridley.com

Little Roni Publishers
ISBN-13: 978-0615656588
ISBN-10: 0615656587 Also available in eBook format

Little Roni Publishers
Byhalia, MS
www.littleronipublishers.com

Cover Photo: Holly Buckingham
Cover Design: Elizabeth E. Little

The following is a work of fiction. Names, characters, places, and incidents are fictitious or used fictitiously. Any resemblance to real persons, living or dead, to factual events or to businesses is coincidental and unintentional.

PRINTED IN THE UNITED STATES OF AMERICA

Join the conversation at #Dirt

For my precious angel

Baby Jade, I love you so much.
You can read this when you're older.

Dirt

Prologue

    The only darkness I've ever known is the tranquil night that flows from moonlight. Now there is another darkness that exists beyond my world of Darby; an evil that lies within the hearts of beings where light cannot flicker.

    I have a feeling things are about to change. Part of me hungers for it; the other part fears my life may be the price. I know this sounds crazy, but because of what I am, my life may be a price worth paying.

1

He traces my shadow. I see his silhouette through the faintly-tinted driver's side window. Making my way off campus, I find Highway 93. I push the pedal to eighty hoping to lose him, then to eighty-five, then ninety. My hybrid is no match for the pristine '67 Camaro. Hands trembling, I grip tighter to the steering wheel. I look behind to see his iridescent black car rushing around each bend. I try to out maneuver him. I can feel the vibrations of my heart as I hold my breath. Although my dad would be upset, a speeding ticket would really be nice at a time like this. Where is the highway patrol when you need them? But if I get a ticket I'll have to explain to Dad why I've been driving like a maniac. That explanation would cause a new set of problems.

My nerves unravel while the stranger trails one or two car lengths behind. I change lanes several times and take side roads, getting off and on the highway in an effort to lose him. *Is he trying to kill me?* My skin tightens when finally the dark car drops off somewhere down Tin Cup Road. Maybe I'm losing my mind, but I know I've seen that car somewhere before.

Dad's car sits in the driveway, so I pull myself together before I go into the house. I can't let him see me upset.

I breathe in deeply as I lean over the kitchen sink. I never thought my first week of college would be this nerve-wracking.

I see it sitting there on the kitchen counter, the glass full of thick yellow muck where I left it this morning. I forgot to take my daily dose. While I watch Dad from the kitchen window as he buries another one of his secrets in the backyard, I chug down the bitter medicine for my condition, "the condition" that doesn't have a name or a symptom. I try to keep from inhaling the horrid scent of the homemade drug as it slides down with three huge gulps.

Dad walks in through the backdoor, unaware of his worn appearance: a tailored button-down and wrinkled khakis with a touch of dirt smudged on his knees. Without the dirt it isn't Dad. "Did you take your medicine?"

"Yeah, of course I did." I roll my eyes. In a couple of weeks I'll be eighteen. I'm all grown up now, but he doesn't get it. I'm the one who takes care of him, but he doesn't get that either.

"Ashe." He lifts the empty glass with yellow film left on its rim. "This was still sitting on the counter when I got home."

"You didn't ask me *when* I took it. Better late than never."

"You can't afford to forget, Ashe."

I don't know why I have to take that nasty yellow stuff he calls medicine anyway. I've been drinking it for as long as I can remember. Asking him why I need it agitates him. There isn't anything wrong with me. I take it to make him happy. Anything to keep him from worrying. I've never forgotten a dose, but the excitement of starting college has the better part of my mind.

"How's school?"

"What?" I respond off guard still shaky from the ride home.

"Is everything okay?"

"Yeah…yeah, Dad. Everything's fine," I answer brushing him off. I'm careful not to mention the black Camaro.

I start dinner and the bizarreness of the day begins to wear off helping me calm down. After finishing the baked chicken and mashed potatoes, Dad heads downstairs to his homemade lab in our basement. If anyone ever found out about it he'd probably be arrested. His lab looks like something out of a Frankenstein movie, without the dead body. *Why couldn't he be a normal father and watch a ballgame on TV?* Glass tubes, flasks, pipes and bowls move chaotically on his large stainless steel table. Cold, sterile, metal panels cover the walls. He looks like a mad scientist with his grungy lab coat and extra-thick glasses. Busy, busy, busy. Happiness meets him in his secret world of formulas and yellow muck, a place I don't think I'd care to visit.

During the day, Dad does research for a local pharmaceutical company. I rarely ask questions regarding his work. The answer is usually something I'd have to swallow later. Sometimes, he asks me to help him when he's working down in his dungeonous lab. If I do ask a question, I get some crazy scientific explanation only he and Isaac Newton could understand. I try to keep my curiosity down to a minimum. "What I don't know can't hurt me," I always say.

As I prepare for the next day, I notice a beam of light charge through my bedroom window. The pitch of darkness surrounds us. No one drives down our road at night. Cars seldom travel down our road at all, really. Besides ours, there are only three other houses in the area, and they're miles apart. I look outside and the moon fills the sky as it gleams off something in the field across the street. A rant of fear ices the chills that run down my back when I see the black Camaro parked in that field. It would have been hard to notice, but the fullness of the moon against the impeccable black paint gives it away. The mystery of the stalker overflows my curiosity and I push my fright away as I bite my lower lip. I have to know who's following me, watching me.

I run from my room and out of the front door. As he speeds away, the high-pitched squeal of tires against the asphalt replace the scent of evergreen with the stench of burnt rubber.

"Who was that?" Dad asks standing directly behind me.

"I have no idea," I answer as I stare down the dark empty road, pretending to be oblivious.

"What are you doing out here? It's late."

"Just getting something out of my car," I lie hoping to keep his questions to a minimum. We go back inside. I say whatever necessary to keep the truth from Dad. Honestly, I don't know the truth at this point. This guy could be a serial killer.

As I lay in bed, I think how I miss the quietude of my previous life, my life before The University of Montana. High school is over and except for Taylie Winston, all of my friends have moved away. Taylie and I have known each other since kindergarten. She's the best kind of best friend; the sister I never had. We do things together, but she can also do what she wants with other people and its okay with me. Jealously doesn't figure into the equation of our friendship.

Everyone else? Well, they couldn't get away from Darby fast enough. I don't know what they're looking for, but I love my safe Montana home. The snowcapped mountains and evergreen woods are breathtaking. I don't think any place else in the world could be half as beautiful. I have to admit sometimes I wonder what else exists outside the world of Darby, but it's easier to convince myself to be content. Suppressing any thoughts of leaving home is the logical thing to do.

Darby is a close-knit town. The fact that I don't know this stranger behind the windshield turns my blood to ice water. I want my boring life back. I don't do well with surprises. Predictability and certainty are my favorite places.

My dad further restricts any thoughts of change. It's always been Dad and me. Sometimes he's like a kid, helpless in some ways and brilliant in others. Things would have been so different if my mother hadn't died during my infancy. He's never gotten over her death. For me, well, it's hard to miss someone you don't know. I don't have a single memory of her.

It's not that I suffer a horrible existence with Dad. I love my Dad and he's been there for me as much as he could be. There are some things, well, maybe a lot of things he doesn't understand. He's a strange man; loveable, but strange. He's scientific; I'm artistic. He's formulas and calculations; I'm color and expression. He has a Ph.D. in Chemistry and I'm majoring in Art. We have a hard time relating to one another, but he needs me. Any dreams of a life outside of Darby are strictly out of the question.

My creative expression is my saving grace and a place to escape. Art fills a void an absent mother has left in me. I'm not blaming her, because without her I wouldn't be here, but I'm resentful that her death left me with an identity of ambiguity.

I notice her picture on my dresser, a beautiful stranger, and her intense teal blue eyes seeping through the picture with golden blond hair draped across her shoulders like silken threads. Etched into the mahogany frame is her name, Nuin. I know her only as my mother, a stranger who gave me life. I'm not trying to sound indifferent, but what I see in the picture is all I know of her.

Dad talks about my mother on very limited occasions. Sometimes, he doesn't make any sense. He talks to her and about her as if she's still here. Anyone else would think his behavior crazy and sometimes I do. I have to look really deep down to find his sanity. With all the unexplainable things going on, I'm starting to question my own.

"Be safe," Dad says, as he always does when I leave the house. His obsession about my health and safety is in overdrive. If he had a clue about the stalker, he would probably keep me home. His fear of losing me makes him irrational, so I make sure I drink the yellow muck before I walk out.

I drive up Highway 93 to Missoula, inspired by the mountain view. The sun in the ocean blue sky warms me with each glimmer. I try to relax, but worry unsettles me.

Half-way to campus, I notice the black Camaro trailing behind me. *Maybe I'm getting worked up over nothing. Maybe he goes to school in Missoula. Maybe I imagined that car last night.* I didn't speed up. I let him follow me as if I could stop him. I keep a check in my rearview mirror and notice he drops off his tag as I reach campus.

I manage to make it through English and History without any major event. I need a break and sit in The Recess, the campus coffee shop. The warming scent of my chocolate mocha helps me unwind.

"Hey, girl!" Taylie shouts from across the room. I jolt spilling coffee on my shirt. We planned to meet during our break. Perpetually peppy with perfect hair and makeup, Taylie looks more like a New Yorker than a girl from small town Montana. If "Guys" were a major she would make straight A's and never miss a day of class.

She sits down shaking her head as if looking at someone from a list of top ten worst dressed.

"Ashe, really. We've got to go shopping." My bargain brand faded jeans with threads dragging the hem make her cringe.

"I'm comfortable," I insist, as I try to rub out the brown spot on my now stained green t-shirt.

"How have your classes been so far?" I ask anticipating my next class, Painting 101, with hopes it would be the highlight of my day. I focus on school and I try to weed out everything else.

"Have you noticed all the guys? I think I'm going to go insane," she says ignoring my question.

"I think you're already there."

Taylie scopes the room like a kid in a candy store with an addiction to sugar. Finding a guy is not on my "to-do" list. I don't need the complications.

"Really, Ashe, so many to choose from." She pans the room as if shopping for a new pair of shoes. An expensive pair everyone would want, but only she could wear.

"You're too much," I tell her.

I didn't even go to prom. Believe me, I heard it from everyone. Taylie tried to fix me up with anybody and everybody. Dancing isn't my thing. I tried to convince myself that the whole idea of dating was lame. Well, I guess most guys at Darby High thought of me as too lame to ask out.

A part of me envies Taylie. Her carefree spirit embraces the social scene. I bury the part of myself that longs for what Taylie has. During most of my middle and high school years, I heard from my classmates about my weird dad and his behavior scared most of them away. The guys in high school got on my nerves anyway. I already had one kid at home, Dad. I didn't need another one

"Really, Ashe, you need a boyfriend."

"Why? I am doing just fine on my own." I'm tired of being pushed. I don't need any issues.

"Well . . . y...y...you just do." She doesn't really have a good answer. Sometimes, she's worse than a guy. Taylie's mind doesn't stay in the same place long. "Check out the blond." By this time she eyes some good-looking, unsuspecting victim from across the endless pool of people. I've no idea which one has become her target.

"Oh my God, Ashe, look at him."

"Who?" I ask unconcerned, tracing the campus map for Anderson Hall, ignoring her as much as possible.

"He's unbelievably gorgeous." She shakes my arm trying to pop it out of socket.

What?" I say annoyed. I look up, as if I have no other choice. I follow her finger as she points from behind her book.

Okay, well, yeah he's probably the most unbelievably beautiful human being I'd ever seen. His thick and wavy amber hair shimmers with each beam of sunlight, every strand kissed by the rays filtering through the window. His face formed from the bust of a Greek god. Chiseled. I mean every feature. Perfect. My body tenses when he stares straight at me with his intense blue eyes. Well, maybe he's staring at Taylie. That would definitely make more sense. I blush as he looks our way. Embarrassed by the attention, I drop my eyes back down to the campus map. *Okay, now I'm acting like Dad.* I can't help myself. I'm sure I appear socially inadequate; uncomfortable with the attention because I'm unsure what to do with it.

"He's looking over here. Don't look. Don't look," Taylie says, as she ignores her own advice.

Taylie has to be the one he's watching. Then, I feel a sharp chill as his eyes meet mine. I look down again out of awkwardness. His eyes pierce through me even though I can't see his face. I gawk at the campus map with hopes of protection from being noticed.

What's wrong with him? Taylie's hair looks like it's been poured from a honey jar as it runs passed her shoulders meeting the middle of her back; fair unblemished skin with rich brown eyes. I mean every guy looks at her. Basically, she can take her pick.

Me, on the other hand, well, I'm common; the complete opposite of Taylie. Long dark hair, black as night, olive skin and dark brown eyes. I'm thin and that's the only thing Taylie and I have in common, and the fact that we are exactly the same height, five feet six. I look a lot like Dad. Strangely enough, Taylie looks more like my mother except for my mother's blue eyes. I have never seen anyone with eyes like hers until now. This beautiful stranger looks at me with my mother's blue eyes glowing from across the room. Chill bumps cover me and I hold my breath for a moment as I realize the emotions I have when I look at my mother's picture.

"I'm gonna be late for class." I need an excuse to leave.

"Same time tomorrow, Ashe?"

"Sure." I clutch my books and head to my next class. I turn and glance back at him, his eyes still on me as I make the corner. Everything moves in slow motion as his face follows mine with every movement defined by the longest seconds I've ever known.

I make my way out of The Recess and stop to catch my breath. Out of my element, I don't know what to do with the attention usually intended for Taylie. The thought of having to introduce any guy to my father makes me uneasy. I'm not usually this dramatic, but there's something unsettling about this guy. To keep my nerves from unraveling, I immerse myself in art. It's always been my safe place, so a have a sense of relief as I head to Painting 101.

I need a place to refocus, but the challenge proves difficult. Professor Bran introduces himself as a newcomer to The University of Montana. He's handsome, but in a mysterious way. When he speaks his lips move like a finely orchestrated waltz. He appears to be in his late twenties or even a well-preserved thirty. He lectures to the class, but I feel he's only speaking to me. His lips move, but I hear nothing, as if I'm watching a silent movie. I don't know what the others in class are doing because I can't take my eyes off him. His metallic emerald green eyes are disorienting. As he examines the classroom, I watch him move back and forth and I can feel him hypnotizing me.

I pull my face toward the desk with difficulty as if my eyes are glued to his, magnetized to the glistening of metal in his face. Words float passed his lips like frost in the air.

"Paint what is in your soul. Due Wednesday."

I've missed the entire class. I look at my cell and I notice an hour has passed. *What the hell is wrong with me?*

I turn to the person sitting next to me. "What's our assignment?" I ask with a red-tinged face.

"It's ridiculous. This class is a joke," he says. "I'm Jackson by the way." He introduces himself as he forces another book into his backpack.

"I'm Ashe. What's ridiculous?"

"This professor. He talks to us like we've never painted anything."

"Well, actually I hardly heard a word," I confess with mortification.

He's in a hurry. "This guy thinks we're in kindergarten. Our house. He wants an 11x14 in oil of our house, but it must come from our soul whatever the heck that means. It's due next week. This has to be some kind of joke."

"Oh," I respond confused, as if I've been slipped a drug.

"Got a class across campus. Gotta run." and he bolts.

"Thanks," I say as he jogs away. He probably thinks I'm stupid, and I'm beginning to think the same thing.

What's wrong with me? Where did I go? It's as if I developed A.D.D. overnight. I call Taylie on her cell as I walk to my car, but she doesn't answer.

I can't get Professor Bran out of my head. The entire drive home I can only picture his porcelain face, his bewitching eyes, his mute moving full lips, his dirty blond hair pulled back tight into a pony tail. I live with my father, so I'm used to strange, but this odd encounter freaks me out. It's more out of the ordinary than my unordinary life.

Everything around me has become more unexplainable. As I pull into the driveway, I realize I never saw the Camaro. If it followed me I never realized it.

I walk through the front door and call out for Dad. He doesn't answer. "Hi, Dad," I say again a little louder. Still, there's no answer so I walk toward the basement.

"Good day at school?" he finally responds passing by me as he walks down the squeaky wooden stairs leading to his sterile world.

"It was fine except for a strange professor I have in my art class."

"Aren't those people a little different anyway?" He's one to talk and I'm one of 'those' people. "What happened?" he asks, halfway interested while he mixes the yellow muck in a beaker.

"I don't really know."

"What does that mean?" he mumbles concentrating on pouring the precise amount of whatever he has from a flask.

"When I figure it out, I'll let you know." He isn't really paying attention to me anyway. His mind is focused on his science. "Dinner will be ready in a little bit. I'll call you up when it's time to eat."

While heading up the stairs my cell rings. It's Taylie. "I see where I missed your call. What's up?"

"Something strange happened in art class."

"What? What? Is it a guy?" Literally, I think men are all she thinks about.

"Yeah, but he's my professor."

"What? Are you kidding?" she says insinuating something inappropriate.

"Really, Taylie, calm down and get your mind out of the gutter. It's like I wasn't there. In class all I could do was stare at him. I sat in my chair the entire class and missed everything. I didn't hear a word he said. The guy next to me had to tell me about our assignment. I was really out of it."

"What's he like?"

"Who? Jackson? I don't know. He's okay. This professor though, I don't get it."

"Maybe he likes you."

"Is that all you think about? Let it go, Taylie. I've got to go feed Dad." She can be so aggravating sometimes.

"See ya tomorrow at lunch." She hangs up without getting a thing I said. Maybe I'm tired and making more of this than I should.

After dinner, I begin work on my project for Professor Bran's class. He wants a painting from my soul. A painting of my home. *How weird. What does that even mean?* I haven't ever had a conversation with my soul, so I'm not sure what he meant. What sticks in my mind are those appealingly toxic green eyes. Before I get very far, that's what starts to appear on the canvas. Deep green and almond shaped. Perfectly formed how an eye should be; impeccable lashes that outlined each sclera whiter than Montana snow. I've painted his eyes without even thinking about it. I don't understand what's come over me. He mesmerized me, leaving me scared and excited at the same time. I've got to get it together to keep from losing my mind. I begin to worry I'm turning into my father.

I throw the painting to the side and pull out a fresh canvas. I agree with Jackson's description of the assignment; ridiculous and elementary. I do it anyway, with those haunting green eyes staring at me from the corner of my studio.

3

I swallow the muck and leave Dad's lunch on the table. I make sure I don't miss a dose especially considering Dad's recent behavior. He's been in a state of worry all week.

"Bye, Dad." I leave without waiting for a response.

After Pottery, I head to The Recess to meet Taylie for lunch. I look a mess covered in clay. Every student wore an apron. It would've been nice if I'd known I needed one. Sometimes, I feel so inadequate. After throwing on the wheel, I went to the bathroom and cleaned up the best I could, but I still look pretty bad.

I sit down in a corner booth and try to hide, from whom I don't know. I guess everyone. If anybody looks close enough, they'll probably think I've been mud wrestling.

The afternoon catches up with me and Taylie doesn't show. The shop is less crowded as the day before. I drink my mocha alone. Well, at least I think I'm alone. I search the room looking for Taylie and I see him, four tables down, the blond guy. With no one standing between us, he stares at me hard. No expression. Nothing. *What is he about?* I wish Taylie would show up, and then my cell rings.

"Where are you? Get your butt over here," I demand.

"I'm not gonna make it. We got out of class late and I've got another one in fifteen minutes," she huffs. "Call me later." She hangs up before I can tell her anything.

Great. Perfect. When I need her, she bails. Grabbing my books, I rush out. He follows behind me as I head for my car. Glancing back every so often, I see him walking unhurried as he traces my steps. *How can he look so calm?* I move at a fast walk, almost jogging. He glides in slow motion. Confident. No smile. No grimace. I'm sure he can see the fear on my face. He makes me nervous, but I don't feel at all threatened. Logic tells me to get in my car and get home, but part of me wants to turn around and walk toward him. I listen to my logic. I guess that's my Dad in me. Standing in front of Mansfield Library, he watches me get in my black Honda. I stare back, but my boldness has no effect on him. I sit in my car and time stands still for a moment. Air and space are the only things separating us.

"Hey, girl!" Taylie opens the passenger door and I almost pee my pants.

"You scared the crap out of me."

"Can you give me a ride? My professor cancelled class and now my car won't crank." She doesn't have a care in the world, ever. It takes her a moment to notice I'm shaking.

"Sorry, Ashe." Her hyperactive melancholy becomes a quieter tone.

Panting, I tried to catch my breath. "Are you all right? What's wrong?" she softly responds while patting my shoulder.

"That guy. You remember that blond guy built like the statue of David?"

"Oh, that guy. Yeah, I remember. How could I forget?"

"He followed me out to my car."

"He walked you to your car?"

"No. He followed me out here. Look, he's standing over there." I point to the front of the library. He's gone. "B… Bu… But he was there. Strange. I don't know what he wanted. He followed me and stood there watching me."

"You're paranoid, Ashe." She's probably right and we brush it off or at least I pretend to act as if it's nothing. We head to Darby.

"He may be strange…" Taylie keeps bringing him up as I try to get the events out of my head. "…but he's still hot."

"Taylie, you have a one-track mind. Don't you ever think of anything else?"

"No, not really." She's coy and nonchalant. "Don't you ever

think about them?"

"Yeah, I do… Definitely."

"Why haven't you ever had a boyfriend then?"

"Think, Taylie, if you had to bring a guy home to meet my father, wouldn't you think twice?"

"I guess when you put it that way I can see what you mean." Taylie knows Dad. He doesn't have the best social skills. Okay, he doesn't have any social skills. He could carry on a conversation with a stranger, but it would be forced and uncomfortable for him and for whomever he tried to talk to.

We don't have any relatives. Oh, there is Mr. and Mrs. Birch. Dad gets along pretty well with them. I've known them my whole life. They're the only other people I've ever met who knew my mother. Dad's obsession with his science, my health and my dead mother make up his world. If I had a boyfriend, I know what it would do to him. I don't know what it would do to me and I'm not about to find out.

"Well, at least he seems interested." The blue-eyed stranger that had my insides turned over has Taylie preoccupied.

"I don't know if he's interested or just a creep." I pull up to the little farmhouse outside of town and drop Taylie off. "Dad's gone to get my car and tow it the shop. Can I hitch a ride with you for the rest of the week?"

"Not a problem." I want someone to ride with, especially now, with all of this strange stuff going on.

"You may have to wait on me tomorrow. My last class is a little later than yours," she tells me.

"Okay, I have some studying to do. See ya tomorrow."

When I look down the highway, emptiness fills the road. So, why do I sense someone watching me?

4

His eyes swallow me up with an emerald glow, like green fire. I make myself pay attention this time. *Am I one of those typical stupid freshman girls that get a crush on their professor, making a total fool out of myself?* The thought of it is nauseating. *Okay, Ashe, get over it. Get a hold of yourself. What is your problem?* This is so out of character for me. I'm sensible. My emotions have never gotten the best of me, until now. Practical. *Pay attention.* As soon as I lay eyes on him, it's as if something takes control of me influencing me, manipulating my concentration.

As he demonstrates different strokes with oils, each movement of the brush is abnormally graceful. His voice is sure and smooth. *Am I the only girl in class absorbed in him?* His porcelain skin doesn't look as perfect today and appears darker since the previous class, but beauty hides behind his eyes and seeps out from the faint wrinkles that weren't there days earlier.

"Hey, wake up sleepy head." Jackson pokes me in the arm.

Dear God, am I drooling? I'm embarrassed beyond belief.

"Oh, I'm awake. Trying to make sure I don't miss anything this time." I try to cover up my obvious intoxication. I attempt to recover what dignity I have left. I wipe the drool from my lip with my sleeve. *Ridiculous.*

"Sure," Jackson responds raising his eyebrows as if I've got a giant "L" tattooed on my forehead. Professor Bran glances at me every once in a while with an unusual smile on his face, making me unsettled. I feel as though he's trying to make me uncomfortable. *Am I thinking that because I want to think that?* I'm sure every girl in the room imagines the same thing. I'm getting on my own nerves.

"Next assignment. I know many of you will think it childish," he remarks glancing toward Jackson as if he knows what's on his mind. "I want you to paint a picture of your family, 11x14, in oil. Due Friday."

"What? Are we in kindergarten? Doesn't he know we need time for this stuff to dry?" Jackson mumbles, insulted by the assignment, again.

"See ya Friday." I walk to the opposite side of the room placing the painting of my home with the others. I wait for the blow as the Professor walks along the wall scoping the students' work.

"Ms. Fair…"

He knows my name. I don't know how he knows me from the other thirty or so students in the class. He looks at my painting rubbing his chin while he ponders. He picks it up.

"Hmmm. interesting. And this is from your soul?" he asks with a haunting silkiness.

"It's the best I could do," I answer knowing what he thinks of my inferiority.

"Shows promise," he whispers. I thought he had to be kidding, but nonetheless, I'm thrilled. At least, today I will leave class on a good note.

Heading to the library to meet Taylie, I keep my eye out for the tall blond. Part of me wants to see him. Part of me is dying to see him, but reason and good sense tell me to avoid him. *What would I do if we start seeing one another?* The thought is unreasonable and out of the question. He could be a nut, a serial killer, a freak. I try to talk myself out of wanting to find out what might happen.

I claim a table toward the front of the library, so Taylie won't have a hard time finding me. I pull out *Romeo and Juliet* and began to read my assignment trying to center my attention on the Montagues and Capulets, pretending to concentrate.

The sound echoes through the library as the chair across from me scrapes sharply against the floor making its mark into the laminate. Looking up, I see him, standing directly in front of me with his flawlessly sculpted hand on the back of the wooden chair. His shoulders are broad, fitting perfectly in his white t-shirt and faded jeans. Every ripple from every muscle shows defining the human body like I've never seen before. He leans his head forward showing ever more his perfect definition. His golden wavy hair is sharp and clean, with every strand exactly where it's supposed to be. He sits down and opens a book that's been under his arm. He lifts his gaze from the pages and walks into my eyes, drowning me in blue.

I shake my head lightly, trying to pull myself out of whatever trance I'm in. I feel drawn to him, but unsure. Still, he makes me wonderfully uncomfortable. It's happening again. It's as if the spirit of a carefree airhead has taken over my mind. *Am I becoming boy-crazy like Taylie?* God, I hope not.

That probably didn't come out right. I don't think Taylie is an idiot, she's my best friend. She sees things through a different pair of lenses. Probably something like sunglasses. Really thick, dark sunglasses. Designer of course.

I try to ignore him burying myself in Shakespeare attempting desperately to focus on the written word; anything to get my mind and my eyes off of him.

I can feel him looking at me, saying nothing. I peer up from the book.

"Hi," he says with a slight smile. His lips curve up a little at the corners.

I'm mute. *Can he tell I'm not breathing?* My heart beats solid up against my rib cage on the verge of implosion. I know it has to be making the table vibrate.

It's all I can do. I muster up one syllable. "Hi."

"Anyone sitting here?" he asks knowing the answer.

"You are now," I respond as if I know of anything else to say and being cool is definitely not my thing. *What does he want with me?* I keep my face down trying to avoid a conversation. I know if I speak it will reveal my awkwardness. I can sense his stare.

"I'm Rowen."

"Ashe," I answer without raising my head. "I've really got to study," I say trying to avoid a conversation, not because I don't want to talk to him, but because I don't know how. Guys like him don't talk to girls like me. It's pretty simple. I'm simple. I blend in and I guess I do on purpose.

"So do I," he responds unaffected by my suggestion that I'm not up for a chat. He slides his book across the table out of the way. He's not here to study.

I try to focus on my text. His scent is warm and refreshing. When I inhale, the feeling of menthol rushes through my nose warming my lungs. I catch my breath again; my lungs are fuller than they've ever been with air that makes me feel like I'm breathing for the first time. He continues to stare, saying nothing. *Does he know my palms are wet with sweat? Does he know my heart is throwing itself against my chest?*

Where's Taylie? This situation is wonderfully awkward. I don't want to leave. I don't want him to leave. As I bring my senses back under control, I'm able to find some words somewhere in my throat.

"What are you studying?" I ask trying to break up my discomfort.

"Mythology."

"Oh," I say looking at the unopened book that is pushed to the edge of the desk. I pause for a moment that seems like days. I'm lost in the vapidity of insecurity; my loss for words makes me look brainless. There's nowhere to hide, so I dig a little deeper and to my surprise more words come up passing through my lips.

"Why were you following me yesterday?" I don't want to run him off, but I have to know.

"I wanted to make sure you made it safely to your car."

"Why? You don't even know me."

"Hey, Ashe. Who's this?" Taylie jumps in at precisely the wrong time, clearly more excited than she needs to be, smiling ear-to-ear. "Rowen, this is Taylie. Taylie, Rowen."

"Isn't this cozy." She's a little too giddy.

"Guess I'd better be going." Rowen glides his book along the table and slides it back under his arm, elegantly floating across the room. The library doors brushes a breeze smoldering him like a blanket as he walks out.

"Okay, details." Taylie insist.

"No details, Taylie. He just came over and introduced himself. No biggie."

"Ashe, you need to loosen up."

Inside, I hope to see him again, but I don't want Taylie to know. She'd never let it go. Taylie chatters on as we make our way through the parking lot. What she says exactly, I have no idea.

I plop into the driver's seat and I see him again, standing on the steps of the Fine Arts building. He watches me. No smile. No wave. Nothing. No acknowledgement that I'm looking at him. It's all so strange. I crank the car and pull out onto the road. Through my rearview mirror, I can still see him standing there watching me as I drive away. I don't let Taylie know he's there. I don't want to hear her overly excited assumptions. She continues muttering about something and she doesn't even notice him. He seems to be everywhere I am. I'm not complaining, but I wish I knew where this is going.

After dropping Taylie off at her house, I stop by the Birches to pick up the meal Lucinda has for us. She cooks dinner for us on occasion and even though they aren't blood relatives they're the only real family we have. Their house is several miles from Dad and me. They've lived there for as long as I can remember, but they go out of town a lot so we don't see them often. I think they have a condo down south or something. They're pretty well-to-do. I pull up to the big flat stone house always with a manicured garden. I ring the doorbell which plays a whimsical melody. The door flies open.

"Come in dear." Mrs. Birch apparently knew it was me. She grabs me and hugs me while squeezing the breath from my lungs.

"Hi." The words barely push pass my vocal chords because of the limited air supply. She's short and round, but stout as an ox.

She pushes away from me, and looks me over as if I'm livestock, checking to make sure nothing is broken. "How are you feeling?" she asks as if I would lie to her.

Before I can respond, Mr. Birch comes from around the corner. He puts me in a big bear hug. Marvin is as short and round as Lucinda, both with flaming red hair and freckles which would make it easy to play dot to dot on their faces. They are both a little quirky at times.

"Ashe, is that you? How's my girl? Feeling well, are we?" *Here they go again. Just like Dad. Why is everyone so worried about my health?* I drink that disgusting medicine every morning like I'm supposed to. I can't remember the last time I've been sick with even a cold.

"I feel fine," I respond trying to get beyond the topic of my health.

"How's school?" Mr. Birch asks.

"Great."

Lucinda comes out of the kitchen holding a brown paper bag. "Bake this up at three hundred and fifty degrees for about thirty minutes."

"Thanks so much," I say as I take the casserole from her. I love it when she cooks for us. I could smell an appetizing scent coming from bag. I'm not much of a cook and her food tastes like something I would imagine my mother making. I head for the door.

"Leaving so soon?" Marvin asks.

"Yes, sir."

"Tell Henry 'hello' for us."

"I will, and I promise I'll stay longer next time. I have a lot of homework to do."

"Of course, dear." Both of them hug me as if I'm theirs to keep, pressing the casserole into my ribs. They're so good to me and that makes leaving them difficult. They're the grandparents I never had.

When I get home, Dad is in the backyard burying something again; the usual for our house where everything is unusual. I shake my head as I watch him through the kitchen window; he looks so consumed with what he's doing. I know he isn't normal. Whatever is in his mind seems to keep him prisoner. I feel sorry for him sometimes.

I wonder if my mother hadn't died, would he have become this? At times, I can hear him talking to her as if she were here in the flesh. He's imprisoned by the love he had for her. Sometimes, I think he's losing his mind, but he's high functioning at work and is apparently pretty good his job. He's received a lot of awards from his research and developed medications that have saved the lives of many people. They say there is a fine line between genius and insanity. Dad teeters on that line every day. I worry one day he'll fall onto the side where he could lose himself.

As I sit eating the vegetable casserole, Dad meanders into the kitchen. Dirt on his pants as usual, bringing with him a musty outdoors smell saturating his clothes. "How ya feelin?" he asks his standard question.

"Fine, Dad." Same conversation. Same tone.

"Your mother is real proud of you, Ashe."

"Thanks, Dad." He speaks as if he's talked to her personally. "The Birches said to tell you hello." I watch him eat. He's in his own little world. Thinking. Conjuring. Creating. I wonder what could be going on in there, in his mind.

I lay in bed resisting the morning with thoughts of his sharp features piercing my mind and the rays from his teal blue eyes burning through me. He smells of evergreen, fresh, and wholesome, but I know that no matter what, Rowen is off limits.

As I wake up, I feel the warmth of the sun hitting my face through the window. My skin is tinged, but comfortable.

"Ashe! Ashe!"

The frantic calling of my name pulls me out of my comfort, out of my thoughts of what might have been a wonderful dream.

"Ashe! Ashe! Ashe!" Dad is in a panic.

"What is it? What's wrong?" I rub my eyes as I run down the basement stairs. His lab is in shambles. Someone broke into the house during the night.

"We've got to call the police." I pick up the house phone and start to dial 911. In one swift movement, he pushes the phone out of my hands onto the floor smashing it into pieces before I can finish dialing.

"No! No!" he insists pacing back and forth running his hands through his dark brown hair that is in wild disarray. He begins dialing his cell phone.

"Who are you calling?" My hands are quivering with the thought of someone being in our house without us knowing it. I slept through it all. The back door to the basement was apparently left unlocked and whomever it was entered at their leisure. There wasn't any forced entry.

"Dad, who are you calling?"

"Marvin, get here as soon as you can. Someone's broken into the lab."

"Why are you calling Mr. Birch?" Dad's face is mangled in worry.

"He'll know what to do, Ashe."

"The police will know what to do." I try to bring him to reason.

"What do you think they would say if they saw a set up like this? How would I explain it?"

I can see his point. He picked up his cell phone again. "Who are you calling now?"

"Into work." He may have been late often, but he never missed a day on the job.

"I'm not going to school today. I need to stay here and help you get things cleaned up."

"Yes, you are. I would feel better if you did. You don't need to miss class. That will give me something else to worry about." He looks up his face caught in an expression of surprise and runs outside into the backyard. I follow behind him. "Thank God," he sighs.

What in the world is he worried about out here? We have a large yard and nothing but national forest behind us. Wilderness. Lots and lots of wilderness. What is it?" I ask confused.

"Nothing," he responds as he goes back inside and I follow behind him. He's keeping something from me. I hope he's not into anything illegal. *No way, not Dad.*

In a fluster, he looks around the basement at shattered glass and upturned tables. He's a ball of nerves, falling apart. Marvin arrives to help with the mess. He's aware of Dad's strange ways and it doesn't seem to bother him. Sometimes, he helps Dad in the lab. I guess they're kind of like kindred spirits. Marvin Birch is much older than my father and has his wits about him.

"It's going to be alright, Henry. We'll get this cleaned up," he reassures Dad, whose hands are still shaking.

I call Taylie to let her know I'm not going to make it, but her car is still in the shop and I don't want her to have to miss school too. So, I listen to Dad and go to class.

"Ashe, don't worry. I'll take care of Henry. Everything will be alright." Mr. Birch gives me a wink, his voice comforting and calm. I would probably be in the way if I stayed.

As I wait in The Recess, I search the room from a corner booth. I hate to admit I hope to see Rowen again. I wonder if he is watching me. He isn't here, but I can feel his warmth in the air which is fresher than usual. Maybe, I'm wishing it, dreaming the air is different.

I have to keep my head out of the clouds. I can't get emotional. I can't let myself get too close to anyone, but I can feel myself getting caught up in the thought of him.

I have Dad to think about, but the thought of Rowen sparks another side of me; a side I don't know. I didn't see him today. *Is that why I feel so empty? Is that why my heart feels bare and exposed?*

When I arrive home I head straight for the basement. "Everything seems to be in order now and accounted for," Dad announces. His lab is back to normal and he's much calmer. He's still sweeping up small flecks of glass from broken flasks off the floor.

"You need to make sure you lock the back door from now on," I instruct as I wonder whom would do this.

"I thought I did. Marvin helped me get everything back together." He tries to capture every speck of glass, as he looks down with each word. Eye contact isn't something he's good at.

Tonight, sleeping will be difficult. I'm hoping the break-in is an isolated incident, but the whole thing has me on edge. I'm able to get my next assignment completed, "The Family Portrait," Dad and me holding a picture of my mother, done in oil, 11x14. I don't see how Professor Bran expected us to paint that in two nights and then only three days for it to dry. He's rushing us; speed painting. I'm not pleased with my work, but I'll have to turn it in anyway.

When I start to fall asleep, I hear the staircase creaking. There's one plank that has a distinct cracking sound when you put your weight on it. It's loose and Dad has never fixed it. I ease out from underneath the covers and go down the basement stairs. Someone is down there. I can hear them moving around. Holding my breath, I continue down the steps and turn on the lights.

Dad and I scream in unison. "What in God's name are you doing, Dad? You scared the crap out of me." He's trying to catch his breath.

"I came down to check on things. Couldn't sleep," he huffs.

"After what happened last night...you had me worried. Don't do that again."

"Sorry, Ashe. I think I'm going to sleep down here tonight," he says as he points to the worn leather recliner in the corner of the room.

"Whatever, Dad. But keep this light on." I turn on the desk lamp in the corner and turn off the florescent lights. I walk back upstairs and back to my room relieved it was only Dad. I stop in the doorway. *What if they come back and Dad is down there by himself?* So, I sleep on the sofa in the den in case he needs me. Watching over him is my lot in life, my purpose and sometimes it makes me feel trapped.

A part of me thinks Taylie really has it made. She's able to do whatever she wants, with whomever she wants, whenever she wants. I feel tears seeping into my eyes, but I don't know why I have the urge to cry. *Only if my mother hadn't died, things would have turned out so differently.*

I've never felt so emotional about it before. In the past, I didn't let myself get emotional about it, about anything. I bury my feelings because life is safer that way. It's easier to accept responsibility, but for the first time in my life I want something else. Something I can't have. Someone I can't have.

Professor Bran stands in front of the class looking over us reeking of boredom. He lectures on the mixing of oils today and we turn in our assignments. Jackson painted a portrait of five cows and a pig sitting on a couch. I have to say it's pretty good. "It's an abstract." Sarcasm reels from him. "The pig is my cousin."

"What do you think Professor Bran will say?" I ask.

"Don't really care. These assignments are ludicrous." Jackson's talent is obvious, so I can understand the reason for his frustration.

The Professor walks toward us, picks up Jackson's portrait and smirks with his right brow raised. He plops it back down on the desk and turns to look at mine which is boring and uneventful. Aesthetically speaking, it's not done nearly as well as Jackson's. This project proves I'm not the best artist in the world, but I do love to paint. Watching the Professor's face, he gives my artwork a quick glance.

"Perfect," he says. I can't believe his comment. Jackson wrinkles his forehead looking my way.

The professor strolls back to the front of the room, collects a black bag from his desk and leaves.

"That fool. He wouldn't know talent if it kicked him in the face." Jackson takes a quick look back at me realizing his insinuation. "No offense."

"None taken." He's right though. Jackson has more talent than most of the class. Anybody could see it. "Don't let it bother you. Maybe, he's jealous. We haven't even seen any of his work yet."

"I can't drop the class. Guess I'll tough it out." And he storms from the room.

I meet Taylie at The Recess, the local coffee shop. She's waiting for me at the table that has become our usual spot. I scope the room, trying to hide my motives from Taylie, but I don't see him.

"Things settle down at home?" she asks.

"Yeah. Still shakes me up a little." I answer scanning the room. He's not here. Well, if he is I don't see him.

"I've haven't seen him either." Taylie must notice my preoccupation.

I don't respond and pull an apple out of my bag attempting to act nonchalant.

"What do you think that was all about, in the library? One minute he's following me and the next minute he's gone," I ask. Taylie knows what's on my mind so there's no sense in trying to hide it anymore and she knows a lot more about guys than I do.

"Guys. You can never figure them out. Don't even try. I wait for the next one to come along." She grabs her stuff. "Gotta run."

Taylie has another class, so I wait for her. After she leaves, I bury myself in Romeo and Juliet. Taylie isn't gone long, and I'm getting into the study mode, when the air around me becomes warmer and fresher. He's here. I can sense him. I look up and he's pulling out the chair across from me, helping himself to a seat.

"Hi, again," he says as if he expected me to be here.

"Have you been watching me?"

"I waited for your friend to leave so we could talk."

"Well, here I am. Alone. Well, technically I'm not alone anymore." I start to babble. My nerves get the best of me again. Palms sweating, heart pounding, and my breath begins to leave me.

"I had to talk to you alone. I heard what happened at your house last night."

What did he say? I'm floored and for a moment scared to death. Chills run down my back and through my gut.

"Who are you? How do you know where I live? No one knows about last night. Did you...?" I tremble as I sense my wooden chair softens like quicksand and I sink. My voice shakes as if I'm sitting naked in below zero temperatures.

"It wasn't me, but I do know who was there."

"Who was it? Who are you?" Everyone looks at me. I guess I'm yelling. "Who are you?" I insist, my voice a little quieter. I catch the polish of his eyes and suddenly fear rushes from me. For some strange reason I feel safe with him, but I'm still angry because he knows something I don't.

"The Birches. They're friends of mine," he explains.

"I've never seen you there." I relax a little more as I lower my voice.

"They told me what happened. Be careful, Ashe. There are....well, there are...people out there who will hurt you. Who will hurt your father."

"Okay, now you're really scaring me. Who are you? And what do you know about the other night? Why are you following me?"

Questions spew from my mouth like word vomit.

He hesitates, "To protect you." He places his hand on my arm and looks down at me.

"Why do you need to protect me? You hardly know me." I rub my arm still warm where his palm had been.

He doesn't disclose anything. "Trust me. Can you do that?" His voice is calm and deliberate, soft but strong, soothing but energizing. I only know his name, his first name.

"I trust you," I say without wavering, without thinking twice. The quivering is gone. "But I would like some answers," I add as my logic decides to become a part of the conversation.

"Not now," he says.

"I've never seen you at the Birches." I don't doubt him, but I try to get some answers and right now it's like pulling nails from hardened asphalt.

"I've known them all my life," he informs.

"What do you know about my father and who would want to hurt him? He's harmless."

"Not now, Ashe. There's so much you don't know." That's obvious.

"If not now, then when?" Dad and I are in danger so you would think I would have a right to know what's going on.

"Be careful," he says still unwilling to divulge information, still moving my pulse in a race it cannot win.

Rowen stands up as I remain sitting, staring up at him. He towers over me and I feel protected, but I don't know why. Taking my hand, he pulls me close to his chest. I stand up gazing into the abyss of blue that has now swallowed my soul. His lips linger without an invitation.

"Ummm, am I interrupting something? Excuse me?" I hear Taylie's chipper voice, somewhere in the background, breaking up the moment. Apparently, she's been trying to get our attention.

"Oh. Hey," I mutter as I come out of a trance.

"We've got to go, Ashe. I've got to go to work." She waves her arm urging me toward the door.

"Oh, s...sure," I stutter.

"I'll walk you to your car." His touch moves down as he presses the palm of his hand in the small of my back leading me away from the table. I sink into his hand and I'm now in unfamiliar territory.

"What are you studying, Rowen?" Taylie asks still bubbling over as we walk.

"Mythology."

"Cool. So where are you from?"

"Hmmm…Hamilton." He doesn't seem too sure of his answer.

My mind races. I'm confused. The logical, reasonable Ashe tries to convince me I shouldn't trust him. But I do even though I have no answers, no conclusions.

We arrive back at my car. I reach for the door handle, but Rowen beats me to it. Smooth as silk and without arrogance, he opens the door for me catching me off guard. His face brushes against mine, shy of touching me as I get into the car.

He leans in. "Be careful," he whispers.

Shutting the door, he steps back and watches us drive away. Taylie is beside herself. "Details, details, details."

"There're no details," I insist.

"Ashe, what happened? There's something obviously going on between the two of you."

"I don't know what to think about it all, Taylie. He knows about the break-in. He says I have to be careful. For Dad to be careful."

"Okay, that's kind of creepy."

"You don't think..." I pause for a moment doubting everything. "He knows the Birches." I remind myself.

"Well, that explains it."

"Explains what?" I respond glancing away.

"How does he know about what happened the other night? The Birches. They must have told him," Taylie says.

Instead of an explanation, all of this raises more questions. My mind drifts off, as Taylie babbles on and on about me and Rowen. It all sounds like chatter in the background of a movie theater as my mind is cluttered with thoughts of his identity. Thoughts of why I'm so unbelievably attracted to him despite all of the unanswered questions make my mind swim with waves of uncertainty. Nothing about this whole situation makes sense. I should be terrified.

On my way home after dropping Taylie off, I become worried about Dad. Apparently, he and I both need to be careful. Something or someone out there wants to hurt us. I want to get home to check on Dad. Driving down Highway 93, puffy gray lines of smoke-like clouds stream over the trees in the distance. The longer I drive, the larger the billowing masses grow. The closer I am to home; the growing darkness of massive clouds fills the sky. This has to be a forest fire and it's getting a little too close for comfort.

As I approach our house my stomach sinks to the floorboard. Smoke is pouring from our kitchen window. I bolt out of my car and run through the front door. The heat forces its way through me like a blade. The kitchen is engulfed in a sea of orange and red. Flames dance around laughing in my face.

"Dad! Dad!" I run downstairs to the basement. I search the entire house while the flames are racing me, but I'm losing. Glowing vermillion takes over each room. Pulling the rim of my shirt over my mouth and nose, I cough through the walls of smoke. The heat swells up around me and the fingertips of smoke wrap around my lungs. I have to get out of here and find my father. As I call out, my breath shrinks. His car sits parked in the driveway, so I know he has to be here, somewhere. A gray haze fills my room.

"Dad!" I scream out again and again. I'm not going to get out of my bedroom the way I came in. The house is falling in around me. I want to find Dad and get out of here alive. *How can this be happening? Who would do such a thing? Is this how I'm going to die?* In this brief moment, I give up. I know this is the end.

I can't get my lungs to work anymore as I grow weaker with each step. My legs fail me as I hit the floor. My body is numb so I don't feel much when I meet the hardwood, slowly turning ash around me.

CRASH! My bedroom window burst open, glass peppering the floor. Standing on the other side is Rowen. The sight of him is blurry. I must be losing my mind while I lay dying. *Why am I imagining him at a time like this?* Crazy, the things you think about when you're about to take your last breath. He crawls through the broken pane and picks me up. Impending death can produce some vivid hallucinations. I feel his arms lifting me up off the floor. I'm not dead. Rowen is saving me.

"I can't leave without my father," I mumble.

His deep voice is reassuring. "Your father is safe, Ashe. I've got to get you out of here." With blazes overcoming us, he carries me through the broken window into fresh air.

As I catch my breath, we watch the blazing blue heat turn everything it touches deep red and orange. The aromas of soot, smoke and destruction pierce my nostrils with the memories of what used to be. We watch as the burning beams plunge to their deaths. With each charred ember, my home falls to the ground. I bury my face into Rowen's chest sobbing out of control.

"Where's my father? Where is he?"

His gentle touch of open palms cup my face as he lifts my gaze with soothing words. "Your father is safe with Marvin and Lucinda."

"Who would do this?" I ask falling to my knees stunned and utterly overwhelmed. Everything I've ever known is dust.

"We've got to get out of here," he says.

I'm taken aback by his urgency to leave. "We've got to call 911," I insist.

"That won't do us any good now."

"What do you mean? What are you doing here?"

He doesn't answer and takes my arm pulling me toward an older model Camaro that looks new. Then it hits me like a ton of bricks. I jerk my arm from his grip. "It was you! Who the hell are you?"

"There's no time to explain. Not now. We've got to go." The sounds of sirens howl in the distance. He takes hold of my arm again and forces me near his car.

"Let me go!" I try to pull away, but I'm no match for him. "What do you want with me?"

"Get in," he says with insistence forcing me into the passenger seat as lights flash in the distance.

"Take me to Marvin and Lucinda's. I need to see my father."

"We can't go back."

"We have to go back. I have to see my father!"

"We can't, Ashe." He looks at me sternly and his voice is loud, almost yelling.

"Stop the car!" He keeps driving, his speed accelerating. "Stop! I mean it! What's going on?"

"You are about to find out who you really are and where you come from."

"I know who I am. I'm Ashe Fair. Are you freakin' crazy?" The car's speed increases, while the engine roars over our voices. The speedometer reaches 110 mph.

I hold on to my door and look over my right shoulder. No seat belt. His speed is now 125 mph. *Okay, I didn't die in the fire. I'm going to die in this car with this crazy person.* I close my eyes tight to keep from throwing up.

With my eyes slightly unsealed, I plead with him, "Please tell me what's going on?" He looks at me and sees fear branded on my face. He has one hand on the steering wheel and one hand on my shoulder. This is the one time I wish he wasn't touching me.

"What do you know about your mother?" he asks flying down the abandoned highway as if it's no big deal. I can't bear to look at the speedometer again.

"My mother? Only that she's dead. She died when I was one, I think. That's it. That's all I know." My eyes close again as I hold on, pressing my back into the cool black leather seats while holding my breath. He takes a turn down an old gravel road without hesitating on the bend, and the back tires spin in an effort to grip the loose gravel. He competes with the speed of light and at this point, I think he might win.

37

"What do you know about my mother? Let me rephrase that. Why do you know anything about my mother?" I ask waiting for that moment when we will crash. He doesn't answer. His speed increases heading the car straight for the trunk of a gigantic tree.

My trust in him wavers. I scream. "You're going to get us killed!"

I cover my eyes with my hands as we race toward the tree. Yards turn into feet, feet to inches. No crash. No sound. No eruption. There's only light, bright light for a split second. I feel like I'm floating. Then, it happens.

8

There's a loud booming blow when the car slams onto the ground. No blood. No broken bones. Rowen throws on the brakes. As I peel my hands away from my face, I can feel my heart pounding in my chest. I'm moving and breathing. I'm not dead.

Rowen is out of the car before I realize I can feel my skin. As he opens the door he reaches for my hand. I step out onto a plush, grassy field. The sweetness of the air opens my lungs. It's like Rowen's scent times a thousand. For a moment I'm speechless.

"Where are we? Is this heaven?" I ask with a strained voice.

"No, but the next best thing," he says with pride. "A place between heaven and earth."

He grins a little. I guess I'm sort of amusing. This place feels comfortable, like home, until I look into the distant sky. That's when I know I'm not in Darby anymore. Two perfectly round, full, lavender moons sit side-by-side beyond snow-capped mountains. The sky is blue and pink with highlights of yellow peeking out through the white rolling clouds. Peace fills me, my hand still in his. He guides me from the car bringing me to a large boulder. I'm dazed. If I'd ever been intoxicated, I guess this is how it would feel. I sit down knowing he's in full control. He sits down next to me.

"Are you sure my Dad's okay?" I ask.

"Yes, I'm sure. Rest a minute. The portal can make you a little shaky when you're not accustomed to passing through." He hesitates for a moment. "Are you sure there's nothing else you know about your mother?"

"Only her name. Nuin."

"Really? No one has told you anything?"

I shake my head.

"That's unbelievable and so unfair," he remarks.

"My father didn't handle her death very well."

"Your mother wasn't human," he blurts.

I turn to him in shock. "W...What? If she wasn't human, what was she? What am I, an alien?" A vision of her photograph gushes through my mind. The one that sat on the mantle. Realizing my home has been burnt to the ground makes my chest feel heavy. *Was that even her?* I study Rowen's face to see if a bit of unhumanly details reveal themselves. He appears human. Well, not really, he looks better than human.

"Your world refers to us as faery folk. This is our home, Durt, the homeland of your mother."

"None of this is making sense." I shake my head trying to absorb every word. He stands up with his broad back facing me.

He begins to explain. "Thousands of years ago, our kind lived on earth, but when humans started to destroy the earth with all their toxic ways we had to leave. Our bodies could not tolerate the harsh environment. We began to age faster. We began to change." There's more, but he's careful. I know he speaks the truth, even though it's hard to understand and hard to believe. If my mother was from this strangely beautiful place, then I'm definitely someone other than who I was raised to believe I am.

The ground begins to shake making my feet feel uneasy. The blades of grass quiver. "What's happening?" I shudder with uncertainty.

"You're not supposed to be here. Stay quiet. Don't say a word." He presses one finger softly against my lips. I look at him with obvious question. I stand up and am about to ask what he means. He situates his stance directly in front of me, pushing me behind with a gentle, but protective gesture. He tries to hide me from whatever is about to happen.

Through the tree line, burst three men each riding giraffe-sized winged horses. They're breathtaking with exaggerated necks and full flowing manes that meet their shoulders. As they race toward us, I can feel tremors travel through my legs, up through my fingertips. They slow to a trot, stopping directly in front of Rowen, lining up side-by-side. Air forces its way from their flaring nostrils. I keep my mouth shut as I was told. If I had any speck of doubt regarding Rowen's explanation of things, it's gone now.

The riders look to be about the same age as Rowen, in their twenties except for one riding the white horse. His innocence is transparent. All are some shade of blond with blazing eyes of blue or green.

The blond riding the palomino turns his head slightly acknowledging us. "Welcome home, my brother." He pauses for a moment looking my way. "I see you have brought the secret to Durt."

Rowen bows his head a little in return. "Yes, Alder, I have. Her safety was in jeopardy."

The horses have a difficult time standing still, picking up their legs which are covered with long flowing hair, and pounding their hooves, rattling the ground beneath me. They wear no reins, bridles, nor saddles, but each horse seems to know the rider's expectations.

"What have you done, Rowen?" the apparent leader of the group asks with a deep voice laced with disdain.

"I had no other choice." Rowen answers.

I step out from behind my towering protector. Each one of them looks at me like I'm from another planet. Rowen told me this was my mother's home. These are her people. It's obvious I'm *that person, that human* and I'm not supposed to be here. Their eyes glare, gawking at me. Yeah, okay I'm from another planet, another realm, another somewhere, but I haven't done anything wrong. Not anything I know about anyway.

"I'm taking her to Ivy's," Rowen says.

"We'll do what we can to keep the news from Arcos, but you do know, my brother, sooner or later he will discover the truth?" I remain silent. It seems to be the best thing to do considering the circumstances. I want answers, but this isn't the time for questions.

The slightly darker blond on the black horse eyes me as if he's trying to harm me with his intense stare. Intimidation soaks me to the bone. *What have I done? What has Rowen done?*

The innocent one, however, gives me a slight grin. He glances at me with a sense of understanding, but says nothing knowing his place.

"We'll catch up with you later." Alder raises his right arm and the others follow behind him causing a thunder as they gallop away. In the distance, the enormous winged creatures take flight, elegant and gracious, owning the radiant sky, rising above the treetops as if they're weightless. The ground is still once again.

"Who are they?" I ask.

"Sentries…like me. Protectors. We are bound to one another. One blood. One brotherhood. One's purpose is also the others. Coll rides the black stallion and Ruis the white mare. Alder, the palomino."

"Who do they protect?"

"Depends on orders. They change from time to time." We share a glance. I'm falling for him. I don't know what to do with my feelings.

"Except for me," Rowen continues as he turns away. "My assignment has never changed. I was chosen at a very young age to be your sentry, to protect only you. Coll has always had an issue with that. He thinks it should have been him."

"I guess that explains why he was giving me such a dirty look. He gave me the creeps."

"Don't worry about him. He's angry at me. He's always angry at me."

"Why were you chosen to protect me and why would I need protecting? I'm nothing. I'm nobody."

He chuckles. "You really don't know anything about who you are. Do you?" I guess my face is blank. "Unbelievable. You…"

"What?" I can tell he wants to relinquish more. "You never told me why you were chosen."

"Well, Arcos believed I had the strongest powers of resistance."

"Who is Arcos?"

"Our king…" He wavers again. I can feel the words building up in his mind. He revisits the whole truth, giving into his thoughts. "He's your grandfather," he spouts. "You might as well know that much. You have a right to know."

"My grandfather," I whisper the words with disbelief. I've never heard those words together. They make me feel my mother was real. I scoot to the boulder behind me, reaching back to feel for it as if I'm blind. I sit quiet for a few moments, taken aback and discombobulated.

He kneels down in front of me and takes my hand. "Are you alright?"

"Yeah...yeah." My voice stumbles. I'm not sure if I'm okay or not. Actually, I feel more insecure than ever. I have no idea who I am or what I am. The secrets about my life are beyond my imagination. Apparently, I'm the secret.

Rowen places his hands on my trembling shoulders. "Do you trust me?"

"Yes," I respond without dithering. "Tell me one thing."

"What is it, Ashe?" His eyes sear me with cerulean heat.

"Is my father really all right?" He told me he was and I believed him. I just want to hear it once more.

"Your father is safe, for now. He's with Marvin and Lucinda, but I don't know exactly where they have taken him. His safety is something Arcos will make sure of."

The beauty of this place is overwhelming and beyond anything human. Its name doesn't do it justice. "Of all things, Durt?" I ask.

"Dirt is from where all things come. We came from dirt, our food comes from dirt, and our air comes from dirt. Everything starts there. Everything starts where we stand." I guess he can see the perplexed expression on my face. "You'll understand in time."

I try to digest everything I've heard and seen. Taking my hand, he pulls me from the giant rock.

"Come with me." I follow as we head back to the car. We get in and head for the forest. The engine purrs. "Why would you have a car like this here? Won't it ruin the air or something?"

"Runs on water," he responds.

"Oh."

"We've taken a few human machines and made them safe."

"Where are we going now?"

"To put this thing away." We drive a few minutes beyond the tree line. The engine is passive and makes little sound. The trees congregate, merging closer and closer together. We stop, as the trees close in around us and I sit motionless in the passenger seat feeling as if we're about to be swallowed up by the forest. The door opens; Rowen offers his hand to help me out. His chivalry is satisfying and pulls me in even more. Walking away, I look behind me. The car is gone and a maze of green completely covers the area where the car had been. We walk out into the meadow, my hand in his. I'm certain of nothing, but trusting him with anything.

I think we walk for hours. The trees are greener than green, the grass thicker than carpet. The verdure is pure. And I thought Montana was the most perfect place in the world. Above us, an eternal rainbow paints the sky with colors I never knew existed. I walk with him, wondering, while questions fill my brain. "Who's after my father?" I finally ask.

"To know that you are going to have to know who you are." He pauses for a moment and seems scared to tell me more. "Your mother is from Durt."

"So are you. I get that already. But..." I say with a little agitation.

With a blink of an eye, a dark cloud comes over us like a blanket of despair, erasing the color from every inch of sky. Any natural movement around us stops. The world is stone still. An enormous sense of gloom overcomes the air which is soured by a foul odor. Rowen clutches my arm. I've never seen him afraid until now. "Run!" he says as he drags me faster and faster along the path.

"They're here." Rowen pushes me up against a huge oak and becomes a shield in front of me, again. Two men draped in black cloaks step out of the shadows.

"Look what we have here," one of them spews. "Rowen, the sentry, protecting it. The great secret." They both laugh at us as if we're pathetic.

"Phagos. You know the code. You and Duir are not supposed to be here. You've crossed the line." Rowen's words are guarded.

"Nor is the secret! There is no code now! Now that you've brought it here, there are no agreements. No codes!" Phagos shouts. His deep voice echoes as his face curls with anger. Their eyes glow bright green much like Professor Bran's, but their faces are dark as if they have severe sun damage. I can tell they once owned beauty that faded away or was brutally taken from them. Their thin, light blond hair dances freely with each movement.

"Leave at once. You are going too far, Phagos," Rowen insists.

"Looks like you are the one who has gone too far, Sentry Boy." Phagos reveals his rotting jagged teeth as he bellows a deep disturbing cackle.

Simultaneously, the two iniquitous men pull long silver swords from underneath their robes. Their polished blades shimmer. My heart hammers as fear grows inside me. Rowen's hands are empty. I'm not any help. I'm the reason we're in trouble. I know deep down he'll do whatever is necessary to keep me from the blade.

"Straif will be delighted to have the both of you. He'll be so pleased. The secret. Here. Finally."

Phagos, being the apparent leader of the two, points the tip of his sword under Rowen's chin, lifting his head up with the knife touching his throat ever so slightly. One small movement will puncture his neck. Rowen stands firm between me and Phagos. He has one hand in his back pocket and one hand on me. Phagos and Duir reach to apprehend. Their swords close in and I see my reflection in Duir's blade. I get a whiff of his rank stench; the smell of rotting wood, mold and disgust. There's nothing else we can do. I'll go quietly.

Rowen releases a handful of sand from his back pocket thrusting it into the air, causing an orange cloud to appear around us. I rub my eyes to clear the smoke. Coughing, I'm caught off guard by the scent of citrus. When the smoke clears, we're at the foot of a mountain looking over the most beautiful valley I've ever seen. A meadow full of wildflowers and blooms satiate every inch of space. The perfume is sedating filling the air with the scent of bitterroot blossoms and chocolate. Phagos and Duir are nowhere to be seen.

"Where are we?"

"Millseu Feraib," Rowen says brushing the sand off his bare arms.

I drift toward the alluring field. It calls me, pulling me like a magnet, a force I cannot resist.

"We've got to get out of here and we're not going through there. Come on, Ashe." He points up the mountain away from the intoxicating valley. He grabs my arm forcing me in the other direction, away from Millseu Feraib. Away from valley that summons me. I've never encountered a force so strong. It vacuums my desires. *Why is he doing this? Why doesn't he want to go with me?*

"We'll never get out. It's a trap!" he insists.

I ignore him. He has to be wrong. How can something so

beautiful be a trap? I'm going and he isn't going to stop me. I pull away from him and head downhill in a trance. Drugged. Inebriated by the air around me.

"Come on." He picks me up and throws me over his shoulder. I fight him with everything I've got, which isn't much.

"Put me down! Put me down!" My fists beat against his back without relent as he carries me up the mountain. By the time we reach the top of the peak, I'm exhausted. He isn't fazed. Not the least bit short of breath. I've calmed down by this time and he sets me down. My mind is clearer now.

"I'm sorry. I don't know what came over me."

"I expected that to happen. Don't worry about it," he laughs his subtle mouth slightly curving at the edges. "You've got a nice right hook."

"I didn't?" I could feel the color of red seeping from my olive complexion.

"Right here." He points to his left cheek, which is adorned with a crimson splotch. It's almost as if he's proud of it.

"I don't remember. I'm so sorry. What happened?" I ask mortified.

"It wasn't you. Don't blame yourself. It's the valley. Once you enter, you don't come out. It's a trap put there by The Dark Thorn hundreds of years ago. No one can destroy it. To destroy Millseu Feraib would mean the destruction of all living things around it. Every plant, every bit of life within one thousand meters of it edge. All of it would die."

"How were you able to resist it?"

"Years of training."

"How did we get there? The last things I really remember were those men attacking us."

"Orange sand. Pixie powder. It'll take you to one of three points in Durt. All of which are dangerous and for different reasons. I chose Millseu Feraib because it's the closest of the three to Ivy's house, but we'll have to walk a while longer." I'm getting tired and the sun illuminating this world starts to set giving the sky a hue of deep orange and red. Small specks of cloud frolic around us as we trek upwards. Rowen reaches out for me "Can you walk a while longer?" As he touches my hand, he touches my soul. I wonder if he knows.

"I'll try." He pulls me from the ground. "What do you mean you chose this Feraib place?"

"When you use orange sand, and believe me it's not easy to get, you have to focus on your destination."

"How do you know what your destinations are? Do the pixies tell you?"

He smiles at me in a debonair sort of way. It's obvious I amuse him.

"What's so funny?"

"You don't talk to pixies. You can barely see them. Orange sand is only issued to a certain few, by authorities higher than me. It's not something you use lightly."

I put my hands in my jean pockets and raised my shoulders up around my neck in a moment of total ignorance. "I guess there is so much I don't know. I..."

"Be still. Shhhh," Rowen instructs, placing his finger over my lips stopping me midsentence. A nearby bush rustles. "Show yourself," he insists.

When the creature steps out of the foliage, my heart skips a beat and my jaw meets the ground.

9

"It's only I, Master Rowen." The creature appears to be half-human, half-rabbit and speaks in an accent that sounds awkwardly British. I know now to expect anything and from the look of things, anything is possible.

"Scout, how have you been?" Rowen grasps the creature around his left furry forearm with his right hand. Scout returns the gesture with his right hand at Rowen's forearm and shakes it. We're apparently in friendly company. Scout's torso is human, but from the waist down, he appears to be rabbit, wearing only a khaki vest and brown fur covering his lower half. His face is human-like except for his massive floppy fur-covered ears and a humanish nose twitching spontaneously without purpose.

"What is your mission, Master Rowen?" He looks at me over his crooked round spectacles. "Is...is...this who I think it is? How could you bring this danger to us?" He takes a step back as if I have leprosy and his nose twitches with even more vigor.

"I had no other choice," Rowen responds. I'm starting to think I'm a contagious plague. Realizing his subconscious display of rudeness Scout takes a step toward me.

"Hello there." The creature bends toward me slightly at the waist and I reciprocate the motion.

"Hi," I return apprehensively.

"Dusk is upon us. Come, you both appear tired. You can rest

tonight in Skewantee, but only for one night. I do not want Straif to find it here." His speech is very formal and proper. He apparently knows I have no idea what he's talking about. "Skewantee would be like...uh... your Switzerland. We have no enemies and I aim to keep it that way." He tilts his head forward in an apparent need of bifocals.

We follow the creature into the forest as he hobbles ahead of us; his gait is much like a disabled kangaroo. On occasion, I think maybe I'm dreaming. This reality is beyond real and more than my consciousness can deny.

As we enter the Skewantee Village, more of Scout's kind emerge from behind every tree, every bush, and every cane hut, entire families, children, lots and lots of children. They're sort of like human children in very realistic bunny suits with detachable rabbit ears, some floppy, some stand straight up. Their eyes are solely on me. Whispers and chatter rumble among the masses. Scout leads us through the crowd into a small, woodsy hut with a roof of cane and thatch.

"Remember. Only for one night. I have a village to protect," he says matter-of-factly.

"I appreciate your kindness, Scout. I have my own responsibilities, as well," Rowen says.

"Sleep well my friend." And the creature waddles from the hut.

A warming fire flickers in the center of the room in a ceramic bowl and woven mats lie on the ground. I sit down on one of the makeshift beds and try to get a grip on the last twenty-four hours. Rowen plops down on the mat across from me, the warming fire between us. An awkward silence fills the room. As I lie down, my eyes focus on the ceiling. Finally, we're alone with no distractions and I want answers.

I make a move to find some reality. "You said this was the home of my mother and my grandfather is, well, the king...so...what does that mean exactly?"

"Your mother was like me. A faery."

That's apparent. I want more. He's still holding back. So, I ask again looking over at him with insistence. "And what does THAT mean exactly?"

"It means a lot. First of all... you are half-faery, half-human."

"Rowen, what's going on? Please tell me. Everything I've ever known and everything I am has been a lie. I've been a lie. I need to know the entire truth. Everything about my mother has been a secret. Please don't do to me what has been done to me my entire life. I have to know the truth," I demand.

Rowen turns away. Maybe, if he does not look at me the truth will be easier. "It's forbidden for humans and faeries to marry. Your existence threatens the entire human race, the entire world of Durt," he says.

I sit straight up, confused. *Do I really want to know the rest? Maybe, I'd be happier living in ignorance, living in denial, living without knowing.*

My voice grows louder. "I've done nothing. I don't have the power to destroy anyone, nor do I want to, so what the hell are you talking about."

"If they get a hold of you, it will be hell." His face glows from the warming embers. "None of this is your fault, Ashe. You're a victim of your own existence." His eyes walk upon me slowly.

I drop my face into my hands placing frustration in my palms. "I'm so confused."

My protector leaves his place in front of the fire to sit beside me. Putting his arm around me, he pulls me close to his warmth as small tears seep from my eyes. There's more than comfort here. I can feel his passion wanting more, but holding back. I try to get control of myself and my emotions which are verging on the edge of a cliff with no end. He pulls me even closer, consoling, but desire is building between us. His body is warm against mine, giving my tears an excuse to subside. For a moment, an energy of security surrounds me.

He slowly removes his arm and places his hands on my shoulders, gently pushing me away as if he has been caught in an inappropriate situation. He looks me in the eye. The passion still there, but laced with an air of seriousness. "I want to tell you a story." I listen trying not to be distracted by wanting him, trying to hear his words, trying to keep my emotions from influencing the moment. His eyes could drown me with the glistening of ocean waves, but I have to be strong. I have to focus.

He sits back and removes his hands from me. "Centuries ago, after our kind left the human world, a boy was born. His father, a faery, went to the human world through the Portal of Feda. He committed the unforgiveable. He fell in love with a human. This woman had a child, a bithling, half-human, half-faery. His name was Luis." He pauses for a moment looking away. "The boy was put to death at the age of eighteen." His masculine voice cracks.

A surge of razor sharp cold runs through my body. "What on earth did he do? What was his crime?"

Rowen drops his head as if in shame. "He was born," he says plainly and without inflection. His face still turned away from mine.

"W...W...What?" I stutter as I start to put things together. *I'm a bithling. My father and my mother...things are looking bad.* I won't let myself think of the possibilities.

"The Elders of the time handed down the sentence with great sorrow. Their hearts were broken by the decision they had to make. To take the life of anything or anyone is against our belief. Durt is a place of peace and life. At least this is what we strive for."

He leans toward me and attempts to look at me again, as he continues to explain. His gaze calms the fears boiling up in me. "Ashe, there are forces in our world evil beyond anything the human world has ever seen, beyond any vile depravity you can imagine. You met two of these forces in the forest before we went to Millseu Feraib."

"Phagos and Duir?"

"Yes, and they are the least threatening of the evil ones known as The Dark Thorn."

"What do they want with a bithling? With me? What can I do to them? I'm no threat."

"When a bithling reaches eighteen years of age their blood becomes priceless and powerful. It holds the key to control all of mankind, human and nonhuman. Straif, the leader of The Dark Thorn, has been waiting for you to reach the age of maturity. The age that could annihilate us all. If a faery eats the flesh or drinks the blood of a bithling, they become immortal in our world as well as your world. They develop powers surpassing anything manmade, anything and everything. The power faeries hold are mild compared to what could happen if The Dark Thorn were to get ..." He stops midsentence. He can't finish his thought in words.

I sit frozen. "They're going to ....kill....?" The incomplete question is forced. Saying the words makes me sick to my stomach. In ten days, I'll be eighteen. In ten days, it will all be over for me.

The woven flaps that make for doors of the tent fly open. "Something to eat?" I jump on hearing the words. A Skewantee female comes in and with her slightly hairy human-like hands places a wooden bowl of fruit and vegetables beside me along with a gourd of water. The moment is silent. I'm thinking the unthinkable.

"Thank you, Lilly," Rowen answers. Her inelegant large paws move out of the tent stepping backwards out of the door trying to be as quiet as possible.

"You are quite welcome, Master Rowen. Both of you rest well." And she's gone.

"That's Scout's wife. She's very mothering. It comes naturally; she has about fifteen children."

I'm not thinking about food at this point. The sickening feeling intruding my gut is overwhelming. My life was so simple in Montana. So predictable. So safe. Now, nothing is predictable. "Luis's story is going to be my story. My tragedy. My death."

Sensing my turmoil, Rowen brushes his hands softly against my cheek. "Your death is what I am here to prevent. I am your sentry, your protector. Your safety and survival are my sole purpose in life." His complexion glows from the fire light. He's seemingly confident of his ability to keep me from the fate he's revealed.

"What will happen to me? Will the Elders have me killed?" I ask wanting more certainty. I want an answer that will assure my safety. My life.

"Your mother, Nuin, was the daughter of Arcos. You are the next in line for the throne of Durt. Nuin went against her father's wishes and broke the law by marrying Henry, but Arcos loved Nuin so much. So, you are why I was chosen. He'll protect you at all cost. There's never been a bithling other than Luis. He didn't survive to see eighteen. You are the only bithling who has lived to this point. So, what your life will be like is a mystery, but I do know Arcos loves you and will do anything to protect you. You need to trust me, Ashe. On my life, Straif will never harm you."

His face is full of passion and his eyes draw me in. He moves closer, his face a fragment of air away from mine. "You are why I was born. Why I even exist. I was chosen at a very young age out of many to be your protector. An honor I don't take lightly." His lips are a breath away. I want to know how his mouth feels pressing against mine. Each curve. Each crease. The moment stands still. I've never known the tenderness of another's lips. His right hand moves down my shoulder rubbing my upper right arm. I linger.

He gives in, his lips full with heat, his gentleness intense, making me want more. With this one perfect kiss, he has me. For the ten longest, most wonderful seconds of my life I am right where I want to be, in the incandescence of Rowen's arms, his body pressed to mine warming me with his. When out of nowhere, he pushes me away hard. Not gently, not with care. He breathes heavily as if he's been running as he tries to pull away from desire. "I can't do this."

"What is it? What did I do?"

"I am your protector. Th...there... are rules. I've trained. I don't understand how..." He bursts up from the floor ruffling the mat.

"What are you talking about, Rowen? What's wrong?" I screwed up by being born and now I've done something to push Rowen away.

As he storms out of the tent, I follow after him. He presses his palm against the flat part of my upper chest below my neck. His fingers firm against my clavicles, "Stay here." I stop in my tracks with his hand up against me. As he approaches the doorway, he hesitates; turning back with a softness covering his face and he pulls his hand away. His voice softens, but I feel a hole bore through my soul. A vacancy fills my heart that isn't supposed to be there.

"It's not you, Ashe. It's...it's me. I'll be outside. Get some sleep." *How can I sleep now?*

There's a price on my head and Rowen has rejected me. On the inside, I'm in a state of panic as everything falls apart. I step back from the door and plop down on the mat. I'm exhausted, physically, emotionally, mentally. I figure besides being alive, I can't do any damage while I sleep.

10

It can't be morning. Darkness fills the room. The small fire from last night is gone. In fact, I'm no longer in the hut. The stench of rot and filth fills my nostrils.

"The secret awakens." A dark sinister voice comes from the corner of the strange room. A man wearing a black skirt that meets the ground and long-sleeved tailored black jacket stands quietly in the corner. There are no windows. Burning torches mounted on the stone walls provide a limited view of my surroundings.

"Who are you? Where am I?" I insist my fear breaking through my uncertainty.

He ignores me. He's on the other side of a set of bars that I check in vain. My fears are confirmed; I'm locked in. His ominous shadow heads off with enthusiasm, like a kid who has done something he's proud of. I sit in the corner dazed and alone. *How did I get here? Where is Rowen? Is this a nightmare?* The slime of my own skin lets me know this is real.

Three men march toward my cell. A tall, lanky man covered in a brown and black cloak unlocks my cage.

"Straif wants to see you." Air passes coarsely across his vocal chords like that of a chain smoker. *Straif, I remember Rowen mentioning him. The Dark Thorn, they have me.* My mind races and panic travels along my nerves instigating the trembling of my hands. Shadows around me reveal themselves. The men all look a lot like Phagos and Duir, dark wrinkled skin, green piercing eyes, long blond unkempt hair, and wearing long black skirts. Two of them grab me tightly, one on each arm, forcing me to my feet.

"Move it," one of them instructs.

"Follow me," the tallest one demands.

I do as I'm told. I've no idea how I got here. The last thing I remember was falling to sleep in the hut at Skewantee.

We walk up several flights of a stone stairwell, narrow, aged, smelling of dust and revolt, with one man in front of me and two men behind me. My pace slows and one following jabs me harshly in the back with a cane.

"Straif doesn't have all day." His rough voice joins the chant of his cane each time it hits the stone floor.

"Where are we going?" I have nine days left before I'm to become their victim, so I thought I'd ask.

"We're going to prepare for your birthday. And what a party that will be," the shortest of the three responds with a wicked sneer and haunting tone.

"A little early don't you think?" Sarcasm coats my words as I ascend up the staircase.

"You'll be eighteen in seven days and we've been waiting for the day a very long time. Everything must be in order." He speaks as if he knows something I don't. As if I'm unsuspecting of their plans. I don't know the details, but I know enough.

Seven days. I thought I had nine days before the dreaded day, my eighteenth birthday. *How long have I been here? Where is here? I've lost two days.*

I'm shoved into a huge room beautifully adorned with enormous pieces of art. Most appear to be early Renaissance and reveal magnificence. Huge columns support the ornate cathedral ceilings. No chairs. No furniture. There's a vacant podium which extends along the full back of the room standing about three feet above the black glistening, polished floors. They're like ebony mirrors clearly capturing each reflection. Specks of light from the torches illuminates the enormous space.

A force pushes me again from behind by the tallest of the three pawns making a surge of pain run from the middle of my back down my side where his thick yellow fingernails pierce my skin through my shirt.

I stumble to the middle of the room. My escorts remain by the door quiet, pretentiously awaiting reward. They're very overconfident. *Is my capture their accomplishment?* I'm helpless, alone, and worried about Rowen. I know this is bad, but it's going to get worse. I'll be eighteen in seven days. I've lost time. Maybe time is different here. *Are the days shorter?* It's possible. Anything is possible.

I'm not feeling myself. While standing here helpless on display, I realize I haven't had my medicine since I arrived in Durt. No one knows of my health problems, not even me. I only know I have one. My unnamed illness may kill me before they do. The thought of the unknown of what might happen if I don't take the yellow muck scares me to death. I've never really had to worry about it until now. Because my illness has never been explained to me, my imagination has no limitations about what would happen if I miss a dose. Death is insinuated. If not death, I know the consequences would be bad. I recall all of those times I complained about the yellow muck, now I wish I had it. In the loneliness of my destruction, I wish I could taste the bitterness of the yellow syrup, the hope it gave me, the peace it gave Dad.

Anticipating the arrival of the infamous Straif, I start to believe waiting is going to be a part of his torture, a part of my suffering.

Crisp against the floor, I hear each footstep distinct and echoing through the massive room. From behind one of the large pillars, a tall blond man with a wickedly flawless face swanks onto the platform. I wouldn't say he's beautiful, because of the evil that evaporates from his skin, but splendor hides underneath what's on the surface. His black robe floats behind him. He is statuesque and sure of his space. Turning to face me, he sits down in one flowing motion, graceful and intentional right in the middle of the platform. He stares at me saying nothing. The massive room fills with deafening silence. I look at the three behind me who wear anxiety in the creases of their eyes. They're obviously unsure of what will become of them now that their leader has arrived.

"It's a pleasure to meet you, my Ashe. Ashe Leigh Fair."

I turn back focusing on the dark voice at the front of the room.

"Who are you? Where am I? What day is it?"

"Whoa, whoa. Wait a minute my dear. One question at a time." He's not endearing. His voice is twisted and infected. He appears to be one who would enjoy a slow methodical torture of whatever victim, whatever sacrifice he may have on hand. Consequently, I'm today's special. "Perfectly understandable that you have much to ask. I'm Lord Straif. Leader of The Dark Thorn. In regard to your second request, welcome to my humble abode, the Conul Cuan Caverns. You've been asleep for two days my dear, so to answer your real question, there are seven days left until the celebration of our life and your death." He pauses. "Unfortunately." His deep voice is calm and straightforward.

I hear the slow agonizing tempo of another set of footsteps enter the room. A black cloak covers the man who makes the sound of hard feet pressing into the black marble floor, and I notice the green emerald glow of his eyes. Professor Bran stands on the podium staring at me as if he knew I'd be here. How did he get here? What was he doing in Missoula? I tremble as I realize he's been a part of this all along. What is his role in my ....my... death going to be?

"Well, well, well. I see you've made it," he says with arrogance. He's proud of himself. I keep my mouth shut. He doesn't have the same effect on me he had before. Now, he's repulsive. His enchanting methods to lure me in satisfied his plan. I'm here and that's all he wanted.

I've got to get a handle on what's going on, what's about to happen. I need to keep quiet and try to figure out what I'm up against. I'm not dead yet. I'm not going to give in to them, not until I have to. Not until it's my only option. Still, beyond all hope I try to remove the speck of doubt seeping through my brain; the uncertainty of what I might become. I'm the sacrifice of all living things. I hope there is a way to overcome this nightmare that isn't a dream at all. There has to be a way to survive. I'm not giving up on life easily. Rowen gives me hope that there is more to life than what I've known. Where is he? Is there even a reason to fight? I relive our moment in the hut, the completeness that absorbed me. He is worth any battle I might have to face.

Straif elegantly rises to his feet.

"Well done, Bran. She arrived in plenty of time."

Bran remains behind his leader quiet and sure of himself. Straif steps off the podium and approaches me face-to-face. He's a skyscraper towering over me. Fear seeps from my pores as sweat runs down my neck. The disgusting scent of evil poisons the air. He revels in his ability to terrorize me, looking me over as if I'm about to be run through an auction, circling me.

"In a few days, you'll change history my dear, Ashe. The world, your world will never be the same. We'll finally have our place." He takes his pale finger, with his long crusty yellow fingernail, and brushes it along my cheek. He leans forward, his dry red lips to my ear and whispers with a long sinister breath making sure I hear him. "Nothing will ever be the same."

Sickened, I remain motionless, too scared to move. He smells of sour, dirty water. The unwashed. The unclean. The stench makes me hold my breath. After he fills me with unrest, he walks away. Bran follows as the leader leaves the room, his black cloak sweeping through the air. The professor gives me one quick glance, his assignment fulfilled as if to say, "I win."

The goons who presented me to Straif take me by the arms, twisting and pushing me toward the door. I move like a rag doll. Putting up a fight is futile. Beyond the tall wooden doors, I follow the steps in which I am forced.

We walk by a huge room filled with small creatures running about, working, moving huge pieces of antiquated ornate furniture, laying out rugs, causing dust to fly through the air, clouding the space. As we pass by the open doorway of the room, they freeze in their tracks catching a glimpse of me. The apparent reason for their duties is preparation for the big day, the day of sacrifice. Their yellow eyes gleam as if they have seen a celebrity. Some perch themselves on tabletops like buzzards in order to get a better look. Their crooked smiles reveal their needle sharp teeth and they appear to want more than an autograph. My eyes capture their every move frame-by-frame, second-by-second.

"Move it," the bulky blond growls jolting me from the moment. "Those imps would have you for lunch if we turn them on you and we have to keep you in one piece. At least for now."

The guard closest to the open door sticks his huge square shaped head into the room and yells, "Get to work, Mongrels!" With that, the hideous wrinkled beasts begin working sporadically. I stand out here in this world of blond beings. It's strange, in Darby, I felt invisible.

As I walk, the tiredness in my legs oozes through and I feel stranger by the minute. There's tingling throughout my entire body, how my leg gets when it falls asleep except this strangeness covers my entire body. I'm feverish. Maybe, I'm getting sick because I haven't had yellow muck in days. Straif may not have me alive after all.

My escorts lead me down the dark corridors with only shades of light offered by randomly lit torches. We descend to lower levels of the caverns. My legs are heavier with each step. I don't know what's happening to me, but I do know I've got to find a way out of here.

I worry something dire has happened to Rowen. *Will I see him again?* I know he won't forget me. Something happened that night in the hut. Something neither of us will forget.

Works of art from every period imaginable line the walls of the huge hallways, from artists I know from my world. Michelangelo, Picasso, Monet. Baroque, Surrealism, Renaissance. I wonder how they acquired them. Some of the pieces cover entire walls, while others are a few inches in diameter.

As we walk down more and more flights of stairs, we make our way through another corridor. Then I notice two paintings, in oils. They're mine. The assignments from Professor Bran. "The Family Portrait" and "My Home." *What are they doing hanging on these walls?* As we walk slowly past them, I pause briefly gazing intently at my homework. Memories of my once beautiful home, with the shrubs surrounding and protecting it bring a sense of peace, but as I stare, the colors begin to move, merging together, morphing into another picture: a picture of burned ashes, destruction, rubble; a picture of darkness and disdain.

I look closer at the picture of the family portrait. Dad is standing by me holding a picture of my mother, the original. As my gaze ponders the oils begin to mix spontaneously on the canvas and I see my father sitting on the side of a bed in an unfamiliar room with his fist under his chin. His brow is wrinkled in worry.

"Get a move on, Secret." I receive a firm push from one of my escorts forcing my back to spasm.

He tosses me into my cage, behind the bars of confinement. Without a trial, I'm guilty of living. An infraction I didn't choose. My entire body tingles. Something is terribly wrong with me. Along with my physical detriment, every inch of my heart is a shallow vacant glass.

I have to figure a way out of this prison. I sit for a while contemplating my dilemma. How can I escape? I don't even know where I am. "Caverns." Apparently, I'm at the bottom of a hollow. My fingers and toes sting with periods of numbness, but fear helps to cover the physical pain.

As a little girl, I was sometimes scared to go to sleep. I would lie in bed and imagine holding my mother's hand as I floated into dreams. She helped me to go to sleep without fear. I needed her more than ever. But she's not here. She's never going to be here.

My mind continues to race until I lose the battle. Darkness fills my eyes and sleep takes over.

Awakening from a deep stupor, I still smell my disgust like the pet of a cruel, neglectful family. I hear chatter coming down the stairwell. "Okay, later," a husky feminine voice responds to someone. A woman covered in black brings dry bread and putrid water.

"Here, Secret. Eat up." Her slick blond hair is pulled tightly in a bun, raising her eyebrows as if she's had a botched face lift. She hands me a cup made of mirrored glass providing me a view of my worn reflection; a reminder of my predicament. I look horrible and I need to go to the restroom. Maybe the female guard will be more agreeable.

"Hey, I need to go to the bathroom."

"Shut it up. You're not coming out of there," she barks. I don't know why I thought she might be more understanding. After all, she is one of them.

She sits outside my cell. I guess she's supposed to watch me, making sure I eat something.

"There has to be a bathroom in this God-forsaken place."

"All right, all right. But no funny business. There's only three more days till ... well, just don't try anything."

Three more days. I must have slept through the last few days again. The way things are going, I'll be dead tomorrow.

The gangly woman unlocks the door and grabs me by the arm. Even with her small frame, she has the same strength as the male guards. She jerks me out and we ascend upstairs.

I take a quick glance at my paintings from Bran's class. As the original work of my family dissolves, another oil illustration comes forth, morphing quickly as colors merge to form an image of me walking up the staircase. Then it dissolves back into the boring image of my previous existence. I stare briefly at the picture of my home, a pile of ashes emerge and then briskly disappear back to the original state of mediocre artwork. As we walk up five flights of stairs I realize the paintings were Bran's way of watching me. He had me paint those pictures in order to keep track of me. That was his role in my capture. The paintings are Straif's security cameras.

My pace slows, preoccupied in thought as we pass the paintings. "Move it." The female guard starts down a long passageway. Almost every inch of wall up to the height of the towering ceilings are covered in art. These pieces, however, don't hold any secrets I can uncover. They hold only beauty.

She walks through a large wooden door. "Come on." I hesitate into the bathroom as she stands there watching me.

"I can't go while you're in here." She folds her arms across her chest. "Where am I going to go? Really?" I guess she doesn't really want to be in here with me either.

"Take care of your business. And make it fast," she says and struts out of the bathroom, her black robe chasing behind her.

I use the restroom and wash up in the sink. The plumbing is different than what I'm used to. The cool water runs out of the rocky walls into a basin refreshing my skin. There are no towels, so I use the bottom of my ragged brown t-shirt. The mirror over the sink is cracked and a vibration away from shattering to the floor, but I'm able to make out the reflection of the window behind me. It's small, but it's still an opening to the outside.

"Hurry up in there!" Helga, or whatever her name is, bangs on the door while yelling at me.

"I'll only be a minute. I'm washing up." I stall for time. I find a long, slender piece of stone on the floor. I shove it in the latch preventing the door from opening. The window is my only chance for an escape. The hammering at the door grows louder as my guard tries to get inside. I climb on the back of the toilet seat and reach for the window latch. There aren't any bars keeping me in. I don't think they have prisoners often. Maybe, I'm the only one they've ever had.

"Open this door!" A man's dark voice insists. I unlock the window and try to pull myself out.

"Kick the door in!" someone yells. Pounding rings through the planks of the wooden door.

I grab the outside window's rim and feel the flesh of my palms tear from a razor sharp edge. Black thorns surround the edge of the window's seal. *Yeah, they've had prisoners here before and this is how they keep them.* Blood streams down my forearms dripping in my face. Pain sears through my hands. Splinters of wood bounce off the door as pounding rattles the room.

My heart sinks when I hear Straif's voice. "Stand back, incompetent fools." And the door blasts open.

Rowen

I was stronger than that, or at least I thought I was. Her kiss was more powerful than any force I've ever encountered. Stronger than any energy I've ever defeated, but more wonderful than anything I've ever wanted. Yes, I failed, but I don't care. I want her. I want all of her.

As I enter the tent my heart breaks. They took her during the night through a fresh slit in the back of the hut. I fall to my knees on the ruffled mat and notice the tracks in the dirt floor. She was dragged out of here. Thoughts of what her condition might be puts a fear in me I don't recognize. Until now, I haven't known how it feels to lose. There's an emptiness inside me; death in the living.

I've got to get her back, but I can't do it alone. By now, the others know. Alder, Ruis, and Coll are probably headed here and I'm sure Coll is happy I've failed. He has to be relishing in the fact he was probably right; only if I hadn't given in to my heart.

The sound of horse's wings announces my brethren's arrival and I'll have to explain myself. The ground trembles as they land.

"What's happened that we've been summoned?" Alder asks.

"They've taken her."

"What? How could you let this happen? I knew it should have been me!" Coll yells.

Coll is in disbelief, but underneath his tone is a secret pleasure. He wants to be in my place so badly, but he has no idea where my heart is.

"I let her sleep in privacy. I left her alone during the night and

The Thorn captured her. I never heard them." Ruis, the youngest of our group remains silent.

"Come, Rowen, we'll return to Congramaid to prepare. We will get her back," Alder instructs. Our brotherhood is known for its strength. Alder doesn't scold or reprimand. "We have to focus our energy on getting her back. We keep the news to ourselves to prevent terror among the people. If those of Durt find out Ashe is in the hands of The Thorn, fear and panic will overcome. Our job is to keep the peace."

I fly with Alder on his palomino, who is a tamer sort. Each sentry is assigned his own horse when he passes through Congramaid. When riding another sentry's horse, one has to be respectful. Otherwise, the results can be tragic.

We head to Congramaid, the training center for sentries and their horses. Although it's good to see home, I need to be with Ashe.

I can't bear to think of someone harming her. A surge of fury builds up in me. I know Straif won't kill her now. It's not yet time, but I'm not sure what he'll put her through while waiting for his indulgence.

I let her down. I promised her I wouldn't let anything happen to her. I remember when I was sent to Congramaid, taken from family, my parents. Emptiness filled me then. I felt so alone. So without. That's how I feel now.

Caring for a female is against everything I've ever been taught. I was taught to love, but not to fall in love. That's like breathing without air; like eating without taste, living without life. I never realized how empty my life was until I met Ashe. Now, she's invaded my soul there's no turning back.

As we fly over Congramaid, younger sentries train in the fields. They look up at us and wave toward the sky. Being a sentry is more than a job. It's a life of sacrifice, celibacy, and commitment to rules. These boys look up to us. A sickness invades my stomach because I'm living a lie, a disappointment to those who appointed me and what's worse—I don't care.

Alder and Ruis load their gear. Saille, the stable master, brushes Ruamna down for me. She's a deep red sorrel, almost a chestnut about seventy-five years old, not quite full grown. That horse knows me better than I know myself. Her back is the safest place in the world; at least it is for me.

Coll struts up, his head held high with shoulders back to exaggeration. He gives me the silent treatment and the creases in the corner of his eyes reveal agitation. I can't really blame him.

His black stallion stomps in place unable to stand still. His personality is a lot like his rider's, edgy, hyper, and constantly moving. Coll is never able to relax. He's always close to combustion, but that's what makes him Coll. Some might call him passionate. I call him annoying. Nevertheless, we're a part of the same brotherhood, and no matter what, we'll be there for one another through thick or thin, life or death, right or wrong. That doesn't mean we have to agree on everything. When it comes to Coll and me, there's no agreement on anything.

"I hope you know what we are up against, my brothers. This is not going to be easy and we have no choice but to be successful," Alder says.

Our leader is the tallest of our brethren. He's slow to anger. Honestly, I don't think I've ever seen him excited. He deals with whatever problem, whatever dilemma we encounter with calm and decisiveness.

"When we get to the caverns we'll split up in twos. I assume that's where they've taken her. They wouldn't risk moving her at a time like this." Alder speaks of her matter-of-factly. "Are you all right, Rowen?"

I guess my feelings are starting to show on my face. Alder trained with us and he's in charge for a reason. His instincts are beyond anything I've ever seen. He has the gift of reading another's feelings, but he can't decipher the feelings I have now. He has never known love. At least, I don't think he has. That has to be a difficult thing to live with—always knowing how someone else feels and having to separate from it.

"Yeah, I'm all right." Coll stares me down as I lie; another thing I took an oath not to do. He knows I'm hiding something. *Does love write itself on your face? Can everyone tell by looking at me?* I know I'll be discovered sooner or later.

We fly for a couple of hours when we meet the peaks of the Li Sula Mountains. Hiding beneath them are the Conal Cuan Caverns. We land in a valley south of the mountain range.

There are several ways to get into Straif's underworld of caves that tunnel for miles underground.

"Rowen and Coll, you go through the east entrance and we'll go west," Alder says. Ruis is young and his powers have not yet fully molded, so Alder keeps him in sight. All faeries have powers or gifts as some call them. But our abilities are ones that originate from our spirit not from physicality.

"Follow me," Coll blurts taking over. I don't argue; it's not worth it. All Coll knows is what I've known; a mission and the Code of Sentries. No one has ever broken the code so, the consequences of my feelings are on untested ground. I hope Ashe is not paying the price for my weakness.

I follow behind my agitated brother, both of us with swords in hands. I will have her in my arms again. I have to.

Ashe

My hands are swollen, red and burning with pain. Infection appears to be setting in. My female security guard roughed me up pretty bad after I tried to escape and now Straif places Phagos and Duir at my door. I'm out of ideas. Maybe dying is the best thing after all. I think of Dad and how he has always been there for me and how I've always been there for him. Every art contest, every skinned knee. *What will he do without me? How will he make it?*

Thoughts of him without me race through my mind. He's already lost Nuin. If something happens to me that will be the end of him. Then I think of Rowen, the only thing finally right in my life. I found what I want and whom I want. I'm not going to give that up.

I've got to get out of this cell. I have one more day until I'm to be killed. My extremities are heavy. In fact, when I look down, I can't see one of my legs. I can feel it, but I can't see it. *What's happening to me?* I need my medication.

After a few moments of hallucinatory activity I see my leg again, my entire leg. I pull from my gut every bit of energy I have and began to scream, yelling at the top of my lungs hoping to provoke some attention. If I can get someone to open the door of my cage, I might have a chance to run or something, a small chance, any chance.

"Let me out of here!" I yell out.

"Knock it off!" a towering figure shouts back. All I see is

Duir's huge silhouette in a curtain of darkness.

"Let me out! Let me out! Let me out!" I continue snubbing constant orders from both guards to be quiet. I'm like the annoying kid in the back seat of a car on a long distance trip. They try to ignore me, but I make it impossible. As I bang on the bars, I continue to shriek. I'm weaker with each and every strike of my hand to the metal rods enclosing me. Attempting to be stoic with indifference, they really can't do anything to me at this point. Straif wants me in one piece and I'm looking pretty bad.

"Shut it up, Secret!" Phagos yells.

"Get me out of here!" My extremely heavy limbs continue to fade in and out of view. Am I losing my mind or am I going blind? My eyes are playing tricks on me. I need that nasty yellow medicine I've taken all of my life. What I wouldn't give to have it now. I can't yell anymore. I can't bang on the bars any more. The weight of my own limbs is more than I can handle.

I hear Straif's voice coming down the stairwell as it bounces off the rocky walls. "What's all of the noise, my dear? I heard the commotion and wanted to make sure things were still in order." His voice is full of wickedness. The words slide off his tongue like a snake sniffing out his next meal.

With a stern look, Straif glances over at the guard standing attentively in front of my cage whose eyes are wide open.

"Make sure she doesn't lose any more blood. We need every drop. I want her in good shape for tomorrow. Do you understand?" His face is about inch away from the guard speaking in a hushed tone. He gawks at me pathetically through the bars. "This will all be over soon enough, my dear." His words make my skin crawl. Turning to Phagos he demands, "Keep her alive."

The massive shadow bows at the waist. "Yes, your lordship."

As Straif strides out of the room and back up the stairwell, he stops at my homework. He rips them off the wall, and tosses them on the ground in front of my cell.

"We won't need these anymore."

I see a painted image of myself sitting in the corner of my cell, bloody and broken. It's like looking into a mirror I wish would crack to pieces. I don't need a reminder of my predicament.

Falling asleep seems impossible, knowing what tomorrow will bring. I hope it won't be painful and tortuous, but I know better.

I'm too weak to fight. I can barely walk and Straif is going to do whatever he wishes. He's apparently been planning this for a long time, probably all of my life. I guess I was born for this. Ultimately, I'm the destroyer. My life will give evil its power. If I was strong enough, I would end it myself before they could have me. Before they can ki..ki.... I'm unable to complete the thought. I try to keep my eyes open until the burden of my eyelids is too heavy and I give in.

I awaken to cheers ringing throughout the cave. Everyone is thrilled about the gift they are about to receive.

In my weakened state the guards take me from my cell. "It's time," he tells me.

It takes two of them to bring me to my feet. "Walk!" the short one bellows.

I stumble a bit. Knowing what is about to happen makes it difficult to move. I tremble in fear. I think I'm more terrified of the agony than the dying part.

Walking through the hallway, I look at the paintings on the walls and wonder how the hearts of these evil beings can hold the appreciation for the splendor of these masterpieces and still have room for malice. As I'm escorted through the main corridor, the cheers and yelling numbs my ears.

I wonder if my mother knew I'd one day be in this predicament. I guess she did. As we pass the dining hall, I take notice of tables with beautiful ornate settings and banners adorning the room in gold and red. The imps are preparing for a feast they'll never forget. They gawk, each with a smirk on their face.

We enter the great hall, the floor a shining sea of blackness. I don't look down, avoiding my reflection. Straif stands at the front of the room with six men behind him all with black robes dragging the floor. Their slick blond hair is pulled tightly back as each strand strains to stay in place. They look like a group of older sextuplets who were spawned from the devil. Phagos, Duir and Bran are among them. Each one expressionless as if they had been warned to keep any excitement to themselves. Straif, on the other hand, is struggling with his enthusiasm, his intensity is apparent. His green eyes are open beyond normality. I don't think he is aware of his huge grin.

Chills run up the back of my neck and ice down my spine. I'm almost paralyzed when I see the executioner's table in the middle of the room; the leather straps that will hold me in place and keep me from running scare me more than anything. Death row, this is what it feels like. I think I'm going to pass out which would probably be the best thing that could happen. I'm unable to walk up to the table so they have to drag me.

"Come on. Move it."

But how can I? How do you walk when you know you're about to die? They pick me up and throw me onto the table holding me down as I struggle.

"Be careful, I don't want to break her." Straif's words hiss across his lips. He reaches out his hands as if I'm about to crumble. I fight as the straps are fastened around my ankles and wrists. I'm not going anywhere, but it seems unnatural for me to simply lie here without a fight.

"Let me go!" I yell.

"Oh, now we can't do that. You'll miss your party, Ashe. And we've been planning it for such a long time." Straif raises his hand and motions the guards away as he walks slowly around the table swallowing his spit as he examines me with his piercing eyes. The guards join the others on the podium, quietly and reverently.

"Today is the day we have all been waiting for! The day of immortality! The day to end all days!" Straif shouts. I can hear the voices of the masses echo throughout the cave vibrating the walls. I guess those allowed to watch were by invitation only and have to maintain decorum. He allows the cheering to go on for a few moments as I struggle with the leather straps in vain.

"Silence!" he barks and all sound ceases; not a movement, not a breath of air. I wish he would get it over with. The waiting is torture. Is he about to do it?

"Just do it!" I demand.

"Very well, as you wish, my dear. As they say in your world, happy birthday, my dear Ashe, happy birthday."

He pulls out a five-inch blade, shining and polished to perfection. I can see every reflection that falls on it. He slits my wrist ever so slowly carving the flesh enough to have a steady stream of blood. The blade slides across my flesh for about two inches as he holds a glass under my arm. I scream out in excruciating pain; a pain that begs for instant death.

"What are you doing? Please, go ahead with it!" I plead. He's going to torture me and make me live through my own death.

"This may take a while my dear," he whispers with excitement as he watches my bright crimson blood drizzle into the crystal glass. I begin to feel dizzy and I hope I'll pass out soon. I close my eyes and try to picture my life before Durt, life with my father, and what would have been with Rowen. The room begins to spin as I become lightheaded. I see my father holding my hand as we walk through the doorway the first day of school. Eating supper. Laughing in the basement lab.

A strange feeling overcomes my right leg and I barely arouse from my hallucinatory daydream. I tussle lifting my head from the table and notice below the knee, my right leg is a vaporized shadow of itself. It's fading away. Did they cut it off? I didn't feel a thing. I bend my right knee and suddenly my leg reappears and it's no longer strapped in. I don't think anyone noticed. Straif stands on my right side facing me with his glowing green eyes glued to the glass of warm red blood. My blood.

I reach deep down finding strength I didn't know I had and somehow I'm able to raise my free leg up and with as much strength as I can find, I kick him in the back of the head. He drops the glass and shatters as it hits the floor. His immortality splatters across the ebony.

He raises his opened hand over his head preparing to hit me. "Why you little bi..." When I see someone swing through the air, whisking Straif away by his raised arm, throwing him into one of the giant pillars at the front of the room. Metal clashes and I see him, Rowen, and the other sentries. I knew he would come for me.

My blood drips steadily on the floor as I start to slip into unconsciousness. Rowen runs to my side ripping off his white t-shirt. He wraps my bleeding wrist tightly with the white cloth and the bloodletting slows. His brethren fight The Dark Thorn sword-to-sword, three on one.

Beyond the walls of the grand room, the crowd screams in panic and bedlam can be heard beyond the doorway as imps screech in anticipation. The room rattles as the creatures try to force entry to engage the battle ensuring my death.

"Hang on, Ashe. We've got you," Rowen says. His eyes still deep blue and loving me with their gaze. Pulling out a knife, he cuts the three remaining leather straps and lifts me off the table of death. He moves fast or maybe that's the room spinning around. He hands me over to Ruis, who whisks me to the side protecting me from the mayhem.

"Take her out of here."

"What are you doing? Don't leave me. You can't leave me."

"You will be in good hands. I have some unfinished business," he says softly.

I pan the room. Blades move back and forth like glitter in the air with lifeless bodies scattered about. Black robes blend into the ebony floor, but Straif is nowhere to be found. Alder is on the platform engaging Bran. With each jab, Alder is quick to the move. Bran's anger seethes, building into frustration as hatred overcomes him. Suddenly, Alder thrusts his sword into the professor's side and he rests on the floor, motionless, dead with his smoldering green eyes open. The glow begins to fade and Alder looks back at us gesturing with a nod for us to leave.

"Happy birthday to me," I mumble under my breath.

"What?" Ruis asks.

"Nothing," I answer. The door to the room is barred and those on the other side beat on it trying to get it in.

"Where's Rowen? I don't see him. Where's Rowen? Rowen?" I ask with panic.

Coll is engaged with Phagos and Duir while the rest of the thorn retreated following their coward leader. Phagos pins Coll up against one of the giant pillars with his sword about to strike. Alder jumps in between the two giving Coll a chance to break free and he's one on one with Duir, while Alder makes mincemeat of Phagos. He's alive, but battered and bloody. Phagos struggles for retreat as he limps away.

"Duir, let's go."

Duir backs away from Alder and the two vermin leave the room. All the members of The Dark Thorn are gone, but those on the other side are about to break through. A sharp high-pitched squeal pierces the air and splinters of wood fly across the room as imps begin dismantling the door. Hundreds of them move towards us like a swarm of roaches with sharp teeth gnashing. They're crazed with anger and hunger.

"Run!" Alder yells.

"We can't leave without Rowen," I insist.

"He's gone to find Straif. He knows what he's doing." Ruis throws a small thin thread directly over our heads hooking the ceiling and we go straight up and out of a window. The scaly gray imps bombard the room and are at our heels as we rise towards the room's ceiling. Alder and Coll are right behind us with the same move. As we rush down the mountain side, the imps squeal pouring out of the window crawling viscously over one another like rats.

The sentries move fast and never look back, but I do. Saliva drools from the imp's mouths. They slow cautiously then retreat into their cave, except for one. He runs until his eyes explode. Blood and flesh spew from his face and a horrible din bursts from his mouth. Eventually, he bolts into a rock and into unconsciousness.

We arrive in the valley underneath a massive tree. "What happened back there? What happened to that creature?" I ask.

"Imps don't do well out here. They dwell in caves. Their eyes will explode if they are exposed to sunlight."

"Where's Rowen? Aren't you supposed to protect one another? How could you leave him there?" I yell at Alder. I imagine what might happen to Rowen with those evil things running around in there.

"Calm down, Ashe. He's fine." He reacts without alarm.

"How do you know?" I'm confused by his calmness, his lack of concern.

"We are sentries. It's our business to know what's going on within the brethren." Alder peers at me as if I'm guilty of something. I realize it's time to keep my mouth shut.

While the winged horses graze, the moment is quiet. The orange and pink hues of the setting sun comfort me as I sit under the colossal branches. Alder and Coll give me snide glances every once in a while, making me uncomfortable.

"He'll be back. He knows what he's doing. Sit and rest. I'm

Ruis by the way," he says bringing me a gourd of water. I drink spilling liquid out from the edges and down my neck. "Slow down a minute. You'll choke," he attempts to take the gourd. My hands are glued around it. "Okay, but slow down," he responds when he realizes I'm not giving it up. "Want something to eat?" He hands me some bread and an apple. Like a barbarian, I rip the bread apart.

Moments earlier, I was being sacrificed. Now, here I'm eating, breathing, waiting for Rowen, and glad to be alive.

The beauty in front of me is deceptive, knowing the battle underground lingers. I sit quietly and wait, but my eyes can wait no longer. Like curtains on a stage at the end of a performance, they shut tightly hiding secrets behind them.

13

The soothing breeze brings me to consciousness. His blue eyes bounce off the curtain of cobalt sky. "There you are," Rowen whispers.

I sit up screaming, "Oh my God!" And I grab hold of him as tight as I can. We're flying. The trees below us look like bushes as I glance over the horse's shoulder.

"Calm down, Ashe."

"I can't look down," I respond.

"This is Ruamna. Say 'Hi' girl." The horse neighs a couple of times. Her wings span out like a bridge across the sky. As I sit in his lap, I remain latched to Rowen and begin to trust the strength of his arms. After I catch my breath, peacefulness surrounds me, but I then realize how disgusting I am.

"I look horrible."

"You look beautiful, but you don't smell so good," he says as he laughs a little. I haven't had a bath in, well; I wasn't sure how many days. I look like I live on the streets.

"Shut up," I say as I begin to calm down. "Where are we going?"

"To your Great Aunt's house. Ivy."

The wind rushes over us like air through a wind tunnel. Coll and Ruis fly in front of us while Alder rides alongside on his beautiful palomino. His eyes cut in our direction with a grimace of concern. For some reason, I get the sense we're doing something wrong.

"Did you get Straif?" I ask.

"No. He ran off. We're not done with him yet."

"How's my Dad?"

"Still safe." He hesitates. "I'm sorry I let you down. I don't know how you can ever forgive me."

"What do you mean you let me down? I'm here aren't I? Safe, with you."

"But, I promised you I wouldn't let harm come to you. Now, look at you."

"Okay, you don't have to remind me. I know I look bad…and smell bad."

His eyes melt. No tears, but the shimmering of liquid filled eyes stare down on me. "I'm sorry." His voice draws me closer to his face kissing me softly on the mouth, warming my entire body.

"Rowen!" Alder shouts. Rowen looks over at him and draws me closer to his chest. "We'll talk my brother, later."

"What's he so upset about?" I ask. Rowen's face is tight, his jaw clenches. He's hiding something. "What is it Rowen? Have I done something wrong?"

"No, but I've done something no sentry has ever done. We will talk about it later. I know I have said this before. Trust me. I don't know if you can, but I need for you to trust me."

"I do trust you with everything," I murmur. I don't understand what's going on, but there's so much about Durt I don't understand. At least for now, I'm happy to be alive.

We soar through the air; the view below is breathtaking. The trees are full and the sky is a quilted blanket stitched perfectly with mesmerizing colors covering the land. Birds fly below us unaffected by the enormity of their fellow aviators.

As we descend, I grab hold of Rowen with my scabbed hands. We drop so fast it takes my breath away. My stomach sinks to the bottom of my feet as we land in a clearing. Once when Taylie and I were younger, we rode the rollercoaster when the fair came to town. I barely kept my stomach contained. This experience is very similar to that rollercoaster.

We gallop through the woods for a while then arrive at a small stone cottage hidden in a thicket of trees. The thatched roof is tall and built into a huge oak tree, looking like a luxury tree house. Waiting outside the front door, is a very lanky, slender, blonde woman. She's older, but unbelievably beautiful. The small hints of light sneaking beyond the canopy of the trees bounce off her and she glows. She illuminates the surrounding space with beams of gold.

"Who is she?" I ask.

"Ivy, your grandmother's sister."

A relative. A blood relative. Before now, I only knew of one, Dad. I'm embarrassed to meet her. I not at all presentable. *What will she think of me?*

The horses are unable to stand completely still. Rowen jumps down from Ruamna's back without effort. He stands below me with his arms open wide. It's a long way down.

"I've got you," he says.

I slide off the giant sorrel's back and drop into Rowen's arms. We are eye-to-eye, pausing to absorb a glance that without restraint will lead to a secret kiss.

Alder, Ruis, and Coll have already gone up to the house. Rowen sets me down. I'm nervous, but his arms feel safe. I don't want to go in and face rejection. I can already tell Alder and Coll have a problem with me. Rowen senses my apprehension.

"Come on. She'll love you."

My balance is tested by gravity. My feet won't move and I fall to the ground. Rowen reaches down to catch me. He helps me up, but I'm unable to stand. Rowen looks down, his eyes filled with shock, like a deer in the line of fire. Below my right knee there's nothing, but a hazy shadow of what was once my extremity. My leg has disappeared again.

"What's going on, Ashe?" Rowen asks as if I have the answer.

"I don't know. So, you don't see it either? I thought I was going crazy." He sweeps me up and runs toward Ivy never becoming winded, never showing the least bit of strain.

"Get her inside," my Aunt Ivy insists. She looks worried, but not surprised. If I didn't know better I would have thought Nuin's picture on the mantle had come to life. She makes my mother real. Her beautiful wavy amber blonde hair winds its way down her shoulders stopping at her waist as her radiant blue eyes distract me. I can't stop staring at her.

"It's going to be all right, dear." Her voice is soft and musical. I wonder if my mother's voice had been the same.

Rowen lays me on the couch and Ivy rushes out of the room. "What's wrong?" Alder asks.

Rowen points to my missing leg. "What's going on Rowen? What's wrong with her?"

"Come with me." Ivy looks at Alder with a shovel in her hand. They rush out of the front door.

"What's going on, Rowen?" Ruis asks. His innocence shows through his childish expression.

"He's probably screwed up again," Coll says, releasing his bottled-up sarcasm. Rowen gets in Coll's face. They are exactly the same height and nose-to-nose.

"That's enough. There's something wrong with her. This is not the time," he growls at Coll.

"When will be the time, Rowen?" Coll asks after a short staring match and he backs away. "There will come a time, Rowen, and this matter will be dealt with."

"Come on, Ruis." The youngest of the group starts to follow Coll outside when Rowen redirects him.

"Ruis, get the medication for her hands." The youth is unsure of his place and hesitates before he does as Rowen instructs.

Rowen kneels down beside me, putting his hand in mine. My leg still has not reappeared and I am feeling weaker by the minute.

Alder walks in through the front door. "Ashe, how long has this been going on?" he asks.

Ruis brings in a bowl. Alder removes my soiled bandages and places my hands in a solution of teal blue water sparkling with glittering light. The pain goes away immediately and the sores begin to heal instantly.

"I don't know. Two or three days, I think. Time seems so different here." Alder removes my hands from the bowl and Rowen dries them off. They look as if they were never injured.

"That feels so much better," I say amazed by the miraculous healing.

Ivy rushes in holding a jar covered in dirt. She sprints passed us into the kitchen. "What is it, Ivy?" Rowen asks.

The stunning regal woman darts back into the room with the jar cleaned off, drying it with a rag. She approaches me with her perfectly-pressed robe flowing behind her in waves of white. She kneels down beside me. "Drink this."

"It's the yellow muck?" I sit up confused. "Where did you get this? Where's Dad?" She has my medicine, so he has to be here.

"Your father is fine. Now, drink."

I'm hesitant. I glance at her and see the blue that reminds me of the mother I never knew. Can I trust her? I look at Rowen standing behind her.

"It's all right. Do as she says, Ashe."

"Is this the same...?" I'm unable to finish the sentence before she interrupts me.

"Yes, dear. We have a small supply here. Your father has supplied us with the serum, but we have only been able to smuggle in small amounts. Straif monitors our every action and we can't let him find out about the serum or its whereabouts. Now, drink up."

As I swallow, I remember Dad and how he mulled over his lab making this most wonderfully bitter formula. What was once a burden is now a much appreciated gift. I hand the empty glass to Rowen. They snicker as if I have geek stamped across my face. Rowen points to my upper lip. Apparently, I have a yellow muck mustache, to adorn my already disgusting appearance. I wipe it off with the cloth I used to dry my hands. With my olive complexion, it's hard for me to blush, but somehow I manage. I look down in embarrassment and I notice a more vivid image of my right leg starting to appear.

"It's working." Ivy's encouraging. She scoots outside again snatching the dirt covered shovel on her way out. I've never seen a person her age move so fast. Well, I don't know how old she is, but I know she's a lot older than my father.

I feel stronger. "What's going on? What's happening to me?" I ask Rowen.

He turns to Alder for an answer. "Faeries cannot live in the human world. So, in an effort to save your mother, your father developed this serum to keep her alive. The human world is so toxic. Our kind will began to age rapidly and die within months if we're without the serum. Unfortunately, your father was unable to perfect it in time to save your mother. He finished it soon after her death."

"I'm part human though."

"You are a bithling, Ashe. Therefore, your father wasn't sure if your body would be able to tolerate the human world either. He's been giving you the formula since your infancy. However, bithlings do run the risk of dissolution."

"What?"

"As a bithling grows, their bodies begin to change. Some turn to sand. Some simply disappear. Others aren't at all affected by their condition."

"So, being a bithling is a condition?" I say with sarcasm.

"I was told there has been only one before, Ashe," Rowen says.

"There have been other bithlings, other than Luis. You and Luis are the only ones to reach the eighteenth year. Your father has kept you alive with the serum. It's by decree from the Elders this information has been forbidden knowledge to protect our world, to protect your world, to protect you. If The Dark Thorn knew of the serum we wouldn't be having this conversation," Alder explains.

All of a sudden, it hits me. "That's what he's been burying in the backyard all these years. He's been hiding it in the ground!"

"It's not hidden there. It's the dirt that gives the serum its power. Your father discovered this soon after Nuin died," Ivy says and then she leaves through the front door with shovel in hand.

Ivy returns with another dirt covered jar. Her pristine white robe has splotches of brown at the hem. After rushing in and out of the kitchen, and drying the jar off with a clean towel, she hands it to me. "Drink up."

As I gulp my leg materializes, becoming more solid and functional with each passing second until I'm back to normal. The second dose revitalizes me.

"Good, it's working," my aunt remarks.

I'm still wearing the same pair of jeans and green t-shirt that's tie-dyed with black grime.

"Is there any place I can freshen up?"

"Sure, dear, the bathroom is right this way." I lift myself off the couch and have a dizzy spell. My legs are working, but I'm still a little wobbly. Rowen jumps up to steady me and walks me to the bathroom.

"I'm not leaving you," he insists hovering over me as if I'm made of glass.

"I'll be okay."

"You're not leaving my sight," he says looking down at me.

We walk down the hallway of the cottage. The walls are made of stone. The ceilings are about twelve feet high. Light seeps through the green stained glass windows providing a soothing emerald hue. Everything meshes with the natural world.

"In here, dear." Ivy points to a bathroom and then goes to another room. As I enter, Rowen follows behind me.

"You're not coming in here?" I say pushing him out of the doorway.

"I told you. You aren't leaving my sight. We've been through this before. Remember in Skewantee?"

"That was different."

I waiver as we share a glance. Part of me wants him to join me, but I really not ready for 'that' yet, whatever 'that' might be. "Really, I'll be fine." I'm walking better now and make my way into the bathroom.

He steps back. "I'll be right outside."

The bathroom is different from what I'm used to. There're no pipes for water flow. The toilet looks the same. It has a seat, but it doesn't have a tank. The sink has knobs for water, but no faucet. There's a quiet knock on the door. "I'm okay."

"It's me, dear." I open the door. Ivy awkwardly scoots passed Rowen who isn't giving up his post. "Here, try these, Ashe. They were your mother's."

She hands me a clean pair of jeans and an old Beatles t-shirt. "My mother's?"

"I kept a lot of her things. You're about her size."

"Thanks."

"Let me know if you need anything else." Her voice is kind and angelic. She leaves me in privacy, while Rowen remains outside.

I am speechless as I hold something that belonged to my mother. She was real.

I take off my nasty garb and step into the shower pulling the curtain closed. The shower walls are stone and there again no pipes, no knobs. It looks like something from another world. Yeah, right, I'm in another world.

I fumble around unable to figure out how to turn on the water. I push on the rocks in the wall, but nothing happens.

The bathroom door opens slightly. "You all right in here?"

"Rowen? I'm naked!" I pull the curtain around me and peak out from behind it and see Rowen standing there with his eyes closed.

"I heard a lot of noise in here."

"I can't get this shower to work."

He opens his eyes and reaches beyond me, his face brushing against mine. Resisting the moment, he presses a single stone into the wall and a water fall begins spraying out of the rocks.

"Thanks," I say with modesty, wrapped in a shower curtain made from something other than plastic.

"Call me if you need anything. I'll be outside."

My body is refreshed, but my mind is drained. I'm overloaded with information about myself, about who I am, about what I am. I remain underneath the water until my palms begin to wrinkle.

"Ashe?" Rowen calls out. I guess I've stayed under this magnificent waterfall longer than I thought.

"Yeah. I'll be out in a minute." After drying off, I put on my mother's clothes. They fit perfectly and it's surreal. I keep reminding myself these were Nuin's...Mom's.

I smell something delicious coming from the other side of the house. I leave the sentries to their discussion, and find Ivy in the kitchen.

"Need any help?" I ask.

"Sure. I'd love some. Here, you can slice up this bread. Stew is almost done."

The kitchen looks a lot like most kitchens in Montana, except for the water source.

Whatever she's cooking infuses the house with a wonderful aroma and I'm starving. We don't talk much, we don't need to. I feel like I've known her my whole life, like family. Then I remember we are family. I'm so unusually comfortable with her.

"Okay, boys, it's time to eat."

Coll and Ruis storm in, while Alder and Rowen stroll in with a little more finesse, calmer and more grown-up.

We sit at the table, Rowen next to me, Ivy and Alder across from us, and Coll and Ruis at the ends. The boys discuss strategic plans for dealing with The Dark Thorn while Ivy stares at me. I'm not uncomfortable, but curious.

"What is it?" I ask.

She looks down at her bowl. "I've never been to your world nor have I seen anyone from your world. I had no idea what to expect. You look so different than us, but then I again...I see Nuin when I look at you."

I blush not knowing how to respond.

"What's dissemination, Alder, and how do you know about it?" Rowen asks, not purposely changing the subject.

"Because of the other bithlings."

"How many?" Coll asks.

"No more than a dozen in the last three hundred years. We haven't had an issue because sooner or later they all died. Luis, as you remember, didn't have the trait. I think he's been the only one without it." Alder turns, to me. "I didn't mean to upset you, Ashe."

"No, really, I'm okay." In the last few days, I've been exposed to a reality I could not have imagined. At this point, I'll believe almost anything.

"Your father is a brilliant man. The serum he created has kept you alive. But, if The Dark Thorn ever gets a hold of you, your father or the serum, it'll be disastrous."

I want to ask the question, but I'm hesitant. "Why didn't they let me die? Why was I given a sentry?"

Everyone begins looking at one another knowing something I don't.

"We've got to tell her, Alder," Rowen insists.

"We don't have to tell her anything," Coll refutes with a loud tone. Rowen and Coll gape at one another as the tension between them multiplies.

"Boys," Ivy says attempting to keep tensions down.

Alder continues, but he's very careful with his words. I'm not sure I want to hear what he's going to say. "Ashe, you aren't like any other bithling. Your grandfather is Elder Arcos, ruler of Durt. Nuin was his only child. His wife, your grandmother, she…" He stops mid-thought.

"What?" I insist while the heaviness in the room grows thicker.

"We really aren't supposed to talk about it," Alder reminds himself.

Ivy holds her face in her palms.

"What good can come out of keeping things from me? Look where lies have led me, where they have led you?"

"Ivy's sister, your grandmother killed herself after your mother died. Ashe, you're all Arcos has left. He couldn't bear to lose the rest of his family. She's the only one of our kind who has ever committed suicide."

Can things get any worse? I know none of this is my fault, so why am I feeling so guilty? The room is silent. Ivy pulls her hands from her face and tears stream down like opened flood gates.

"I'm so sorry, Ivy," I say, although it won't undo the past.

"None of this is your fault, Ashe. You've been through so much yourself. Don't blame yourself." She's reading my mind. The problems of this world are my fault. I'm the destroyer. Everyone at the table is solemn. As we eat, there is a hush about the room.

I help Ivy clear the table and clean the kitchen while the guys sit in the den discussing strategy. Ivy and I make small talk and then she brings it up.

"I can see you have feelings for Rowen," she says.

"Yes, I …I do," I stutter not sure about where this conversation is leading.

"Ashe, I can understand your infatuation."

I don't appreciate someone I hardly know telling me how I feel. I put up my defenses.

"I'm not infatuated. It's more than that."

Anything I liked about her is now going out of the window. I'm not a child and all I've been through in the last week or so is enough to make me realize what I want. Life is too short. Many of the people in my life who should be here are gone-my mother, my grandmother, and who knows where my father is. I'm not wasting another day pretending the things I care about aren't important. There are a few more moments of silence as I dry another dish and place it in the cabinet.

"There are rules in Durt. Rules made in order to keep peace, to keep order in our world," Ivy says.

"Well, I'm not from Durt. I didn't ask to be here. I didn't ask for any of this. Everything has been taken from me, my home, my father, my mother, everything. Rowen is the only thing that makes sense to me if anything makes sense at all. He is the only one I have right now, the only one I want. I won't give him up. You can keep your rules."

Out of my frustration, the plate in my hand barely avoids breaking when it hits the counter and I storm out of the room, giving Ivy no chance to respond.

Rushing through the living room, I swarm by the guys and

slam the door to my room. I'm not the type who has fits, if you want to call it that, but I've had enough. I plop face down onto the plump bed and scream my anger face down into the crisp linen pillow. I'm done with the lies, the secrets.

"Ashe?" Rowen stands in the doorway. I don't think he knows what to think. This is a side of me he's never seen. It's a side of me I've never seen.

I end the outpour and lay on the bed looking up at the ceiling, seething with irritation. Rowen lies down beside me, turning on his side. His face hovers over mine. "Ashe, you know how I feel?"

I'm not sure what's coming next.

"I know a lot of this makes no sense to you."

"You're wrong," I interject. "None of this makes sense. My entire life has been a lie. Now, I'm in another world, not knowing what I'm supposed to think or feel. I don't know the rules and basically I don't care about rules anymore."

The setting sun beams through the green-tinted window pane casting a glowing hue over Rowen's face. "When someone is chosen to be sentry, he's not allowed certain things. Falling in love is forbidden."

"That's crazy," I say confused. "But why?"

"We are commissioned to protect. We aren't allowed any distractions, nothing and no one to complicate our objective."

"So, I'm a complication."

"You are more than a complication," he responds while the corners of his mouth curl up highlighting his strong jawline. "You're an obsession. My obsession."

He places one hand on my face and the other hand behind my neck pulling me in, kissing me softly until my lips are satisfied.

"You're everything to me. I didn't know what living was until I found you. For so long you were a name, an assignment. The minute I laid eyes on you I felt something different. I tried to ignore it, but it was stronger than me."

He studies my face, tracing his finger tenderly down my cheek. He turns on his back letting out a breath of frustration.

"What will happen now?" I ask. He's at a loss for words.

"Well, Alder and Coll are concerned and feel betrayed or at least I think they do, but they can't really understand our situation. I don't expect them to."

I watch confusion riddle his face.

"I thought you could read one another's minds."

"We can't read one another's mind. We do sense one another's circumstances. If one is in danger the rest of the brethren will know it and I guess Alder and Coll sense a difference in me. I really don't understand anything I'm feeling. So, I can't expect them to be able to relate to any of this. I know I'm a disappointment to the brethren. No one has ever questioned the rules of sentry life. No distractions. Full commitment. It's not something I chose. It was chosen for me."

"Who chose this life for you?" I see his confliction and I'm sad for him.

"It's something you are born into. I was born with the characteristics of a sentry, or so that is what was said and I was assigned at an early age. My parents were thrilled. I was given up to Congramaid when I was about five years old. I was fine with it. I love my parents and still see them on occasion, but Congramaid has become my home, my family." Sorrow hides behind the shallow tears glazing over his lenses.

"I know you are special." I inch my body closer to his, uncertain of my intentions. "Why a sentry? You were a child."

"My parents and the leaders of our village recognized a trait of resistance; the ability to resist pain, evil, greed, all temptation. I've been in training all of my life. But...." Concern shows in the bend of his brow as he raises himself up on the bed. I move back.

"But what?"

"I never expected..."

"What is it, Rowen?"

He looks at me surprised, as if he's never seen me before. "I never expected to meet you." He speaks as if he's disappointed in himself. "I guess I'm not as strong as they'd predicted." He brushes the back of his hand to my cheek and curls up beside me as I rest my head on his chest.

"I'm sorry, but how do they think you can love others and never fall in love? It doesn't make sense."

"Being a sentry requires selflessness. We sacrifice for the good of others, always putting others before ourselves. In order to do that you must love, but falling in love is considered a selfish act." He squeezes me in closer. "You come before everyone and everything now and according to the brethren that's a distraction. A complication that could put others at risk."

I drift off to sleep in his arms, my head resting on his chest, his heartbeat as my lullaby.

Alder knocks on the door. "Hope I'm not disturbing something," he says waking me up to an awkward atmosphere. Sunbeams warm the room.

"What is it?" Rowen asks with squinted eyes avoiding the resplendent rays of light.

"We've been summoned. All of us." Alder gapes at me. Apparently, I'm a part of all of us. He closes the door behind him.

Rowen jumps out of the bed. "We've got to go."

"What's going on, Rowen?"

"We're going to appear before Arcos, your grandfather. I knew this was coming sooner or later." He's concerned, but unexpectedly calm.

"What do you think he knows?"

"Everything." He leans down, gently kissing my forehead. "It's going to be okay," he reassures and leaves the room. I lay on the bed thinking of meeting my grandfather. This should be an exciting time, but for some reason I'm terrified. The possibilities of what might happen. Are we going to be punished?

As I lay here pondering, I see an old white wooden dresser on the other side of the room with the initial 'N' carved on the front of the second drawer. It's not artistically done, but looks like something a child would do to claim her property. The worn paint is uneven, but I guess that's what gives it character. I prod over to the antiquated furniture and trace the engraving with my finger. *Nuin*. It was my mother's dresser. An iciness bites through me as I pull open the top drawer. The wood squeaks as it rubs against its tracks. It's filled with worn faded jeans and old t-shirts. I sift through them and pull out a change of clothes.

I struggle to open the second drawer. I pull harder and it pops out. Soft plain white gowns lie neatly folded. I sift through each stack without disturbing the contents. At the bottom of the stash is a gray marble box about half the size of a small shoebox. I pull it out carefully to keep the sound of my intrusion at a minimum. I know I'm snooping, which is totally out of my character. I carry the heavy box over to the bed worried I might drop it. After setting it down, I remove the loosely fitted lid with dubiety, uncertain of what I will find. It's like meeting my mother for the first time. My mother's box of memories, the closest thing to her I will ever have.

A photograph of Dad and Nuin is the first thing I see. Dad has his arm around her and they are smiling. I can almost hear them laughing young and carefree. Dad's thick, black hair is shoulder length. He wears bell-bottoms and tie-dyed t-shirt sporting a peace sign. His face is full of life, nothing like the man I know now, withdrawn, preoccupied, and secluded. Nuin appears much different in this photograph from the one that once sat on our mantle. There is cheer in her beautiful face. The photograph I remember displayed a woman veiled in sorrow.

I continue to forge through the box. A dried, red rose lay beneath the picture. The fragility of the bud is obvious, so I'm careful not to disturb its rest. Beside it sits a leather necklace with an oval shaped stone pendent, about the size of a quarter, with a symbol engraved in the center of it. Its shape is a backwards "E."

There is a knock on the door. "Ashe? It's me," Ivy says.

"Wait a minute," I quickly respond. I place the lid back on the box and shove the necklace in my back pocket. I put the box back into its secret place. I try to push the drawer back in, but it's hesitant. "I'm coming," I shout again. As I push the drawer closed, it squeaks. I hope my invasion isn't given away. As the drawer closes the door begins to open.

"Did you sleep well?" Ivy pokes her head through.

"Yes, ma'am. Come in." I try to hide my surprise.

"I see you found something fresh to wear." She sits on the edge of the bed, lifts the navy blue t-shirt to her nose and breaths in deeply. "I can remember the day she met your father. She was so happy."

"How did she meet my Dad? I mean she lived here in Durt. Dad was in Montana."

"Your mother was a carefree sort. As a child she was always

happy and extremely curious, almost to a fault," she chuckles. "Arcos and my sister, they could never say 'no' to her. On Nuin's eighteenth birthday, Arcos gave Nuin a key to the human world. Nuin went back and forth from this world to yours. Never with incident. Until... well, until you were born."

There it is again. "My being born screwed up everything," I remark.

Ivy takes my hand continuing to explain, "There're only two keys that open the Doorway of Feda. One key controls entry through the doorway from our world. The other controls entry through the other side, from the human world. Arcos had both keys until Straif stole the sister key, the one that controls entry into the human world from Durt. Nuin was in the human world at the time and Straif locked the doorway. Nuin tried to use her key to return, but it was useless. Straif had locked her out, however, after you grew closer to your eighteenth birthday Straif unlocked the doorway. You were going to be the one who would satisfy his lust for immortality. It was also Rowen's time to find you and protect you. Arcos has never forgiven himself for Nuin's death or your grandmother's death. He's always blamed himself. That is why Rowen was chosen. You must understand your feelings for Rowen will only obscure things. It brings back so many memories of Nuin and Henry. She loved him so much, but that one relationship has jeopardized the existence of our world and your world."

Puzzlement is sketched on my face.

"It is all going to be all right, Ashe. You are here now and you are safe. Your grandfather, the sentries and I will do everything we can to keep you and your father protected." She reaches under her white robe. "I have something for you." In her hand is a small cube about the size of a child's building block. It's made of mirrors, but instead of my reflection iridescent colors dance around the surface.

"What is it?" I ask.

"I know we probably didn't get off to a very good start. I want to give you something only I can give you."

"I'm sorry about yesterday," I say.

"As am I," Ivy responds. "Yesterday, I felt as if I was talking to Nuin. You are so much like her. More than you know, Ashe."

She places the cube in her palms and visions of my mother begin to appear on its surface. "Hold out your hands," she instructs.

I unfold my hands, palms facing up. "What is it?"

"Close your eyes," she says placing the cube in my hands. "Empty out your thoughts."

"What is this supposed to do?" I ask.

"Shhh," Ivy sounds. I try to clear my thoughts.

With my lids shut tight, visions of my mother began appearing in my mind. I see her as a child with my grandparents. Images of her and my dad getting married surge through my brain. She's happy and joyful. I don't know how long I remain in this state, but when my mind goes dark I open my eyes. The thoughts are still in my head as my own, not as if someone told me these things. These memories are as if I experienced them myself.

"Memories. My gift to you."

"Thank you. Nuin, is so real to me now."

"It is my gift. I can store other people's memories, but only if they are given to me. This is a memory cube, much like a CD in your world, except that it can record memories and copy them from one mind to another." She slips the cube back under her robe.

"After Straif locked the Door of Feda, I never saw Nuin again. So I don't have any memories of her after that. Those were sad times for her and not something you would want to recall. I'm not sure exactly what memories will surface, but overtime more of them will be known to you."

Ivy gets up from the bed. "You need to get ready. We'll be leaving within the hour. Oh, and don't forget to take you medication."

"Thanks, Ivy, for everything."

"You are welcome, child. Don't forget I will always be here for you." She eases out.

I clean up, change my clothes, and go to the kitchen where I smell something ridiculously wonderful. Ivy made muffins and fresh squeezed juice. Although it's orange in color it isn't orange juice. I finish my breakfast and drink the muck.

"Thanks for breakfast. It was delicious," I say as Ivy enters.

"You're very welcome, my dear." She's gracious.

"Where is everyone?" I ask.

"Tending to the horses and getting ready to go. It'll take most of the day to get there." Ivy wraps up what is left of breakfast and packs several jars of my medicine. "We have to pack as light as we can. We have a long day ahead of us. You will need to carry a few changes of clothes. I don't know how long we will be there." Ivy hands me a canvas bag.

"Thanks," I say as I head back to my room and pack what I can.

"Everything all right in here?" Rowen asks.

"Better now," I say. He walks up behind me while I pack and puts his warm arms around me, kissing the back of my neck with a softness I didn't want to end. I turn around to face him wanting more.

"It's time to go," he says.

"That isn't fair," I say a little irritated. "You can't come in here and start something you can't finish."

He kisses me again slow and long, but not nearly long enough for me. "They're waiting. We've got to go, Ashe." He takes the bag off the bed and we head out.

Ruamna kneels down on her front legs, bending her knees to the ground for Rowen to mount. He reaches for my hand swinging me up. Ivy rides on the back of Alder's palomino. We take flight, heading straight up almost vertically and my throat sinks to my stomach and I experience the rollercoaster once again.

As we fly, I glance down over the forest and villages. No interstate, no highways, only green vegetation. The homes blend into the scenery and are sometimes hard to pick out. Occasionally, when we glide low enough, people on the ground wave as if they know who we are. Alder and his crew are kind of like celebrities.

"So, how do you like Durt so far?" Rowen asks.

"Well, besides being tortured for several days and being on the hit list of a psychotic, demonic faery who wants to sacrifice me so he can have immortality and universal domination, I guess it's pretty good. After all, I do have you."

"I'm being serious, Ashe. Do you think you could live here?" he asks apprehensively.

"I don't have a home to go back to, except for…"

"Except for what? Your father?"

"Yes, I worry about him. What would he do without me? How would he manage?"

Ruamna dives down a few feet and I squeeze tighter around Rowen's waist. The wind blows my hair into my face, and Rowen reaches behind and brushes it away.

"He's here, Ashe."

The wind rushes across his words. "What?"

"Your father is here."

"How could you keep that from me?" I slap him on the back.

"Did you say something?" he chuckles.

"Is he okay? Why would you keep something like from me?

"He's fine. I'm telling you now, because I found out before we left Ivy's. No one knew. His place of hiding is highly confidential, for his safety and for yours."

"Where is he?"

"I don't know exactly."

"I don't believe you."

His lips curl enough to make me want him. "Yes, you do."

He's right I do believe him. I trust him explicitly. But he doesn't realize how helpless Dad can be. When I was in first grade social services visited our house. Someone reported that my father wasn't sending me to school with proper meals and no lunch money. What they didn't know is that he didn't send me to school with lunch at all. I grabbed whatever was in the kitchen and took it to school. I didn't realize I had to eat certain things to be "acceptable."

Dad wasn't purposefully neglectful. He was different and I realized that early in life. I heard what others said about him, but I knew he was a good man. I knew after the social worker's visit I was going to have to take care of myself and make sure I made things look "normal."

We fly for hours, floating through white clouds that wrap around us like warm blankets. I'm getting tired. I rest my head on Rowen's back never really falling asleep, but as comfortable as I've ever been. Being close to him is the most wonderful feeling in the world. *If Taylie could see me now.*

"Ashe, wake up," Rowen says.

I'm only daydreaming. "What is it?"

"We're here." In the distance I see an enormous structure made of white stone. The bright sky reflects against it making it glow against the green grass.

As we descend, I hold my breath. The drop is steep and it makes me queasy. We hit the landing hard and I hold on as the ground trembles. A crew of rather short men and women gather around us and take hold of the horses as we dismount. They're stocky with wild fire engine red hair and freckles. As they bow to each sentry, they give me a look of uncertainty.

"Hello, Master Rowen." One of the Birches look-a-likes bends at the waist, greeting Rowen.

"Bendel." Rowen returns the gesture as we head for the castle. Bendel looks rough, with his bright red beard braided down to his knees. He wears a pair of overalls and laced up boots.

"They all look like Marvin and Lucinda," I whisper.

"Leprechauns."

"Do what? You mean Marvin and Lu...?"

"Yeah. The human world has distorted who they really are. They do have powers for fortune, but they are probably the kindest of beings. Nuin became ill, and Straif decided to unlock the doorway, but she was too ill to return. Marvin and Lucinda were sent to help. After she passed away, they decided to stay and help raise you. Henry wasn't in any shape to raise a child after Nuin died."

I look behind me as we walk away from the stables. The little people scamper about busily tending to the massive creatures and unloading our bags. I think of the Birches and about how much they've done for Dad and me.

Continuing toward the towers, I notice the clean fresh air that has been a part of my experience. Butterflies, the size of dinner plates, and massive dragonflies swarm around us in a peaceful state of flight. Unfortunately, the tranquility around me isn't enough to calm my nerves. I'm about to meet my grandfather, the king. Rowen holds my hand as we follow Ivy and the other sentries. We ascend up the white stone stairs leading to magnificent wooden doors. They open on their own as we approach.

The white marble floors glisten. Enormous ceilings are supported by massive marble pillars crowning the room. As we enter a leprechaun hurries to meet us. "Master Alder, Ms. Ivy, welcome to Acrimony. Please follow me. His lordship has been expecting you."

His short legs waddle down the hall keeping a pace equal to ours. My hand trembles in Rowen's, as we enter a dining hall with a table that seats twenty.

"Please." The man pulls out a chair, and gestures Ivy to sit. "Everyone have a seat and his lordship will be with you momentarily." He bows and exits the room. We sit at the table waiting in silence for quite a while. The awkwardness and boredom become annoying.

"What do we do now?" I whisper to Rowen.

"We sit and wait."

"For how long?"

"Until he lets us leave."

"Excuse me?" I ask.

"Arcos is here. He'll reveal himself when he decides. Be patient," Rowen calmly instructs. I sigh in attempt to stay calm. What are we waiting for? He called us here. *Is he watching us?*

Moments later, food is brought in and we're served a warm soothing soup, fresh baked bread with butter. Vegetables and fruits release their scents as they are placed on the table and everyone eats intently.

No one says a word and I follow along. At the far end of the table, a man appears sitting in the chair farthest from us. He slurps soup from his bowl. His white hair is braided in one long strand and reaches to his waist along with his braided beard. Still, the room is quiet except for the slurping and clinking of utensils against china. No one looks at him except for me. He sits in an elaborate armed chair and no one seems aware of him. I peer into my bowl eating the last spoonful. When I glance back down at the far end of the table, the man is gone.

"Looking for me?" a deep-throated voice asks.

With the blink of an eye, the peculiar man is sitting at the end of the table closer to us. Everyone continues eating, as if they were in a trance totally oblivious to the old man and oblivious to me.

"Are you my grandfather?"

"Yes, my dear, I am."

"What's wrong with everyone? Can't they see you?"

"Not yet, they're enjoying their meal. I'll invite them to join us in a moment." His grey eyes stare at me with a tenderness I've never felt before. "You don't look anything like your mother, but then I can see her in every inch of you."

I don't know what to say, so I sit here insecure of what is to happen.

"My dear, Ashe, I'm truly sorry for the situation we've put you in. I've tried to protect you, but it seems The Dark Thorn wants your blood as much as I want your safety."

"What will become of me?"

"Of that I am not certain, but I can promise I will do everything in my power to protect you."

"The soup is delicious," Ivy comments uneventfully. She's coming out of whatever spell she's in and the others begin to join reality.

"How long have you two been talking?" Rowen whispers in my ear.

"Long enough to introduce ourselves, Master Rowen," Arcos answers.

"Yes, my lordship."

"I'm sure you know why I have summoned you here. The Dark Thorn is thirsty for the blood of my granddaughter. Her protection is of the utmost importance. However, there's been a breach in the code of sentries which has placed her blood at risk."

Coll gapes at Rowen, with a grin of delight. Everyone knows what Arcos is referring to.

"In order to protect Ashe, in order to protect our future, we must face Straif head on. We will not be able to depend on one sentry alone to protect her anymore. This will have to be a group effort."

"My lord, I ..." Rowen stops midsentence by the raising of Alder's hand.

"The celebration of Congramaid is in five days. We'll be there with Ashe. Straif will come. We'll take him and his men down," Arcos says with confidence. "I'll prepare our people and those at Congramaid."

"Master Rowen... Ashe, I wish to speak to the both of you alone," my grandfather orders. As we leave, those remaining stare down at their plates avoiding eye contact as if they know something we don't.

We follow him through a long corridor, into a room of green and gold. "Sit," he instructs as he points at two high back chairs covered in green velour. He sits facing us.

"Master Rowen, do you know the gravity of the trespass you have committed?"

"Yes, my lord, I do."

"What a great disappointment this is to me. Look at her. My daughter, my own daughter, broke the laws of nature, and my own granddaughter will possibly be the destruction of the world. Have you not learned from this? Have you not learned from anything?" his voice thunders across the room.

"Hold on. I'm sitting right here. I thought you cared about me, Grandfather. I'm your flesh and blood." The old man can't look at me, breaking my heart even more. "Have I brought that much shame on you?"

He turns away. I want his acceptance, but I want Rowen more. "I'm Nuin's daughter. I didn't ask to be born. I didn't ask for any of this, but I love Rowen and I won't let him go."

"He has been removed from his position." He faces Rowen as he gives his orders, but the old man avoids any eye contact with me. "Rowen, you are exiled from the brethren. You must leave at once." Rowen isn't at all surprised.

The door opens and two men stand waiting. "Come with us."

As Rowen walks away, he turns and gives me a reassuring look. I know this isn't the end of things. This isn't the end of us. I want to scream, but I know my ranting would do nothing to help. I feel exactly as I did in the first grade. Alone, but totally responsible.

The man they call my grandfather, is nothing more than a coward. He doesn't want to hear our side of the story. He doesn't want to understand anything more than his mind already believes.

"You couldn't control my mother and you can't control me." I say as I get up from my chair. He looks down to keep from facing me. "Can't you even look at me?" I'm not about to beg for his acceptance, nor his approval, law or no law.

A small, redheaded woman in a floral dress and apron meets me at the door. "This way," this she says as she escorts me to a massive white room, with floors covered in white, marble. I lie on the bed and gaze out of the stained polished glass window. I realize wherever he is, Rowen is looking at the same two lavender moons adorned by the same beautiful stars in the same sky. I'm tired of living my life as if I exist for everyone else. I realize now what happens to me can affect the existence of everything and everyone. But if I'm going to live, there has to be something in it for me. That something is Rowen.

The door rattles. "It's me." Ivy enters, but I continue to stare at the walls with indifference. "Ashe, you know he loves you?"

"Who?"

"Arcos, your grandfather."

"He couldn't even look at me." I turn my eyes toward the night sky. "Where did he send Rowen?"

"To be with his family. A week's ride from here."

"To face humiliation," I add.

"He's old and set in his ways, but he does love you. You remind him so much of your mother. He doesn't want to lose you, too."

"He can't lose something he's never had."

Ivy knows I've had enough. I'm tired of listening to excuses. At this point, I don't care about anyone else's feelings. I'm being selfish and it's about time.

"Get some rest, dear, and we'll have tomorrow to prepare for Congramaid." She kisses my forehead with a mothering gesture and leaves me to fester in the annoyance of my circumstances.

I know he'll be back for me.

15

The castle bustles as everyone prepares to leave for Congramaid. Coll won't leave my side. I'm vexed by the way he hovers over me, as if he has something to prove. He's exactly where he wants to be, in Rowen's place. No one will ever have the space in my heart that's filled by my true defender.

"You'll be in good hands," he says smirking. I do my best to ignore him, but his pride covers him like mud.

"You keep your hands to yourself," I respond. I make sure he knows where I stand.

He towers over me, his beautiful blond hair strapped in a ponytail like a strand of velvet. "I'm here to protect you. Nothing more."

"Rowen will protect me."

"He's in exile. He can do nothing."

"We'll see," I say with poise as I lean back against the barn. My lack of commitment to the mission and to the brethren's plight rubs him the wrong way.

"Rowen broke the law. You have no idea what it means to be a sentry." Coll's jaw clinches as he stares down into my face. If he's trying to intimidate me it's not working and I think that angers him even more.

"And you have no idea what it means to be in love. And you will never know, because you are so in love with your laws." The skin on his face tightens. "I feel sorry for you, Coll. You are empty and you'll always be alone."

Fury builds in him like a volcano. If steam could come out of his ears, smoke would fill the barn.

"You bithling," he says with degradation.

"I may be a bithling, but apparently my blood has the power to destroy you and everyone else," I remind him.

He lowers his voice and peers in my face about an inch away from the tip of my nose. "Yes, but you can so easily be destroyed." He walks away, fair complexion beaming red with irritation.

I watch the fanfare going on around me. Leprechauns scurry about preparing for our flight. All of this is because of me. How I wish to be human again. But I was never really human in the first place. I never belonged. And I still don't.

The ground rumbles as Ruamna pounds the ground in her stall. She's not going anywhere. She's being punished too and for no reason. The other horses are groomed, prepared to leave. The massive sorrel is frustrated, wanting her master. She knows something is up.

A huge white winged horse, larger than any of the others, is lead from his stall by several leprechauns. Iridescent scales covering his flank look like mother of pearl. He's regal standing with his head held high, proud.

Arcos, glides toward the stable in a long, flowing white linen robe, his long, white hair flowing behind him as it's carried by the breeze. A stable hand snaps his fingers toward the ground and Arcos walks up what seems to be invisible stairs to straddle his horse.

Everyone has mounted; Coll rides up and reaches down to pull me aboard. "Let's go." I hesitate to follow his direction.

"Let's GO," he says this time with more demand. I concede and without effort he lifts me onto the black stallion. Coll is as beautiful as Rowen. In fact, they have many of the same features, but Coll's beauty is buried by his personality. He's obsessed with becoming the one who'll save the world. I'm nothing, but a trip down his road to heroism. I hold on to his waist to keep from falling. His body is firm and masculine. I sense the definition of every muscle under his black t-shirt, but touching him makes me uncomfortable.

Arcos is behind the crew on his magnificent stallion, whose mane is so long rider and horse appear as one as they fly. He's nothing like a grandfather, at least not how I think one should be. A cold sense of disconnection and vapidity shroud him. When I found out I was to meet him, I wanted his love and acceptance. I wanted to be a part of someone who was a part of my mother, but after our meeting, I realized he doesn't care about me. Protecting his world from my existence is his only concern. He seems lonely, but comfortable that way.

The sky is our highway for a good part of the day. The air is cool. Coll's horse follows behind Alder and Ruis. Coll and I don't speak. I only hold on to his narrow waist out of pure necessity. In the distance, I see a crimson flag perched on the top of a castle's pinnacle. Congramaid. As we get closer, I see thousands of people on the ground. Either the Congramaid celebration is huge or they are preparing for a huge battle. We land behind a colossal white castle, away from the crowd.

Coll's feet hit the ground hard. He holds his hand out to me and I refuse it. I attempt to dismount on my own, but as I come off the back of his black stallion, Coll grabs me around my waist on my way down; our faces catch a glimpse of one another. He pauses and stares at me, his hands still around my waist. Coll's arrogant demeanor softens for a brief moment. His glance waivers as gentleness seeps beyond his eyes into mine.

I'm uncomfortable. I push his hands away, ridding myself of the awkwardness. Coll then quickly realizes the discomfort of human feelings and his foul manner returns.

He reaches into the bag that's draped across the horse's back and pulls out a brown cloak, complete with a burly hood. It looks like something a monk would wear-a monk with bad taste.

"Put this on," he says as he throws the robe at me.

I do as he says. He grabs my upper arm and pulls me up against his side. "Stay close," he orders. Staying close to him is the last thing I want to do. In a reflex movement, I try to jerk my arm out of his hand, but his hold is too strong.

"What's your problem, Ashe? You aren't going anywhere. What are you trying to do, get us all killed?"

"No, I'm trying to get away from you, but I feel more like a prisoner than a secret." I mumble as we continue to walk toward the

Congramaid Castle. His fingers press into my arm as we follow the others. We forge on toward the castle's arched entrance. Sentries surround Arcos shielding him from the masses who want to get a glimpse of the king.

A young man, dressed in an emerald green satin robe meets us at the door, acknowledging my grandfather's presence with a subtle nod. "My lord, we've been waiting for you. This way," he says as he leads us down a long corridor.

We walk on pristine white marble passing palatial columns perching the ceiling thirty or forty feet above us. The sound of our footsteps resonates against the walls. We weave down several other hallways each one narrower than the last.

"In here," he urges.

We enter a quaint room full of people. Green and gold fabrics drape the walls. As we enter, all eyes are on us. Arcos is escorted to a huge throne at the front of the room. Ruis and Alder shake arms, with others about the room. Ivy follows Coll as he herds me to the back of the room his hand still latched to my arm. I am covered in brown burlap, otherwise, I would stand out amongst the blond hair and fair skin like a lit up billboard. If anyone sees me then the secret will be out.

Alder stands at the front of the room and calls attention to the crowd. "I'm sure all of you have heard rumors of the bithling that has come of age. I'm here to tell you the rumors are true." Rumbling emerges from the crowd.

"Quiet everyone," Alder yells.

I scoot inches behind me until my back hits the wall, pulling the hood of the cloak toward my face to further protect my anonymity.

Alder continues, "The bithling is here in Durt."

"What?" several in the group shout.

"How could this danger have been brought upon us, Alder?" another sentry exclaims.

"Calm down." Alder tries to gain control of the room.

"This bithling must be put to death!" a voice in the crowd shouts.

"Death to the bithling! Death to the bithling!"

I want to hide even more, but there's no place to go.

Alder fails to contain them, as the chanting continues, until a very small sentry dressed in a purple cloak steps on to the platform. He stands beside Alder.

"Cy," Coll whispers with a tone of regret.

"Who is he?" I whisper back.

"He knows you're here. He can feel your presence. It's his gift. We didn't think Cy would be here," Coll informs.

"The bithling... is here! It is here in this room!" he announces. The room grows silent and everyone looks around not knowing what they might see in the ocean of people.

"Alder, where is this bithling? It should be destroyed," the little man speaks as if I'm vermin.

Arcos rises from his chair, moves toward the front of the podium, approaching the crowd of men. The silence in the room is deafening.

"No harm is to come to her. She is to be protected to the fullest," Arcos continues. Mumbling around the room stirs once again. "Silence!" The walls shake with Arco's resounding demand. "If anyone harms..." his eyes wander toward me as he pauses. "If anyone harms my granddaughter they will suffer death." The room roars. What my grandfather has done took everything he had. To be able to admit I am his flesh and blood, he had to swallow his pride, his title, and most of all his fear. *Does he truly care for me? Was I wrong about him?*

"Everyone quiet down!" Alder attempts once again to contain the room.

Arcos returns to his chair. The room contains itself.

"Straif is after the bithling. My brethren have been to the Caverns and rescued her once. He won't stop there. She has had her eighteenth birthday, so he wants her now more than ever. It is a time of great celebration here at Congramaid, but this is also a time of planning. We must make preparations to go against The Dark Thorn. We'll meet again tomorrow before the celebration."

The sentries mumble amongst themselves. Alder pulls Cy aside. The room clears and Arcos is escorted out. Alder and Cy approach me.

I remain covered under itching burlap, my face hidden by the oversized hood. I want to be kept a secret for as long as possible. As Alder and Cy move closer, my muscles tighten as anxiety becomes my second covering.

Cy is about a foot shorter than me, but intimidating. He peers up at me. "So, you have finally arrived... Oh, dear...what will become of our world?" His mousy, feminine voice is sullen.

I pull back the brown hood. "I didn't ask to be here. I didn't ask to be born," I respond in defense.

"Nor did we invite you." His words are laced with acid.

Alder intercedes, "She was brought here for her protection as well as our own."

"The only way we can be protected is if she is dead," Cy responds.

"This was Rowen's project." Coll couldn't wait to put his two cents in.

Alder sneers, "Rowen was commissioned for this at five-years-old. Her protection was determined eighteen years ago."

"He put us all in danger by bringing her here."

"Enough, Coll. He did what he had to do. There will be no judging here. She is to be protected and so shall we protect."

"Your mother has no idea what she has done to Durt," Cy adds.

"Leave my mother out of this!" It's bad enough that he's bashing me, but my mother is off limits. I have my hand on the chair behind me, and it begins to vibrate for no apparent reason.

Alder senses the tension building between me and the little man. "What do you foresee?" Alder intercedes.

While Cy stands there with his eyes closed in a trance, I whisper to Ivy, "What's he doing?"

"He has a gift. A magnificent gift. He sees the future, not everything, just some things."

"He's coming here," Cy says after a few minutes of deep thought.

"Who?" Coll asks.

"Straif."

"When?"

"I cannot be certain, but he will be here. I must go to my chambers and stay focused. No interruptions. I will report to you what appears to me." His eyebrows twist in contempt as he turns away.

"Go, Cy. I will stand a guard at your door to keep you in seclusion," Alder adds. "Coll, you will remain with Ashe."

Ivy pulls the oversized hood back over my head and we

proceed down a small corridor. Ivy's quarters are across the hall from mine. Coll places his hand into my back, urging me into a small room that looks more like a dormitory. There are set of twin-beds and two old wooden desks in the corners of the lifeless room.

Coll follows in behind me. "What are you doing?" I ask, annoyed by his presence.

"I'm staying with you."

"I don't think so," I insist.

"You really don't have a choice in the matter."

"It seems I don't have a choice about anything,"

"Remember what happened last time," Coll boasts, holding his chest up in the air like some kind of body builder.

I sit on the bed and look at him from across the room. "Well, I do have a choice in the topic of conversation and Rowen will not be one of them. In fact, there won't be any conversation."

"Oh, are you going to act like you are five and give me the silent treatment?" Coll says amused. I don't respond. "Fine, then keep silent. Suits me fine." I don't care if he thinks I'm being childish. This will give me a break from having to deal with his venomous attitude.

After a couple of hours of sitting in total silence and with nothing else to do in this empty space, Coll attempts to stir up a chat. I sense a slight flicker of compassion in his words. "Look, I know this has to be hard for you." He's waving a white flag; however, it seems to be a small one.

I'm cautious. I know what he's like. I look over at him, as I lay on one bed and he on the other. Then I turn my eyes back to the ceiling with nothing to say, my face flat and empty.

"You've got to understand the reasons for our actions." He sits up, frustrated he's not able to convince me.

"Everyone here wants to kill me. Everyone except..." and I stopped myself. I remember my rule and I wasn't bringing him up, not with Coll. I don't want him bashing Rowen anymore.

"We have reasons."

"To kill me? Really, Coll. I'm supposed to be okay with that?"

"I don't mean that."

"Then what do you mean?"

"You threaten our very existence. If Straif gets a hold of you...If everyone decided to be like your mother and break the law, there would be bithlings running around like mice. How would we be able to protect them all? Straif would surely succeed."

"So, now I'm a rodent. Why don't you focus on destroying Straif instead of me? He's the real threat. Get rid of Straif and your people will be free."

"It's not easy, Ashe." This is the first time he's ever called me by name.

He is morose as he lies back on the bed staring at the ceiling. He doesn't know what else to say. That's a change. He seems to always have something to spout back with.

After a few moments he takes a different tone. "Females… You're all such a mystery."

"That's an improvement," I say with a reel of sarcasm. "I've gone from mere bithling to female. That's the real mystery."

"I've never been alone with a girl before."

"What?"

"I've always avoided females, to avoid temptation. I didn't want anything to get in the way of my position. Falling in love is forbidden and I intend to keep it that way."

I don't respond. Surprisingly, I empathize with him. In the human world, I always avoided boys, not because I had to, but because it was comfortable. I didn't want to have to confront my father with that issue.

I wake the next morning. Coll sits by the window gazing out. "What time is it?" I ask.

"Late. Almost noon. "

"Did you get any sleep?"

"Sleep? Are you kidding?" He stops himself. "Sorry. I promised myself I would lose the attitude."

"Thanks, I think."

"No. I didn't sleep. I watched over you last night. I can't do that with my eyes closed you know." Coll is so different from Rowen. My blood flows warmer as I think of him. Deep in the core of my heart, I know he'd be here if he could, and that fact begins to stir worry. Has something happened to him? Where is he?

"Get cleaned up. We are meeting with the other brethren in a few minutes."

I raise my hands in the air, shrugging my shoulders.

"Oh, the bathroom is right here," he says pointing to the next room that has no door.

"I'm very aware of where the bathroom is. Do you mind?" He turns his to face the opposite wall. "I mean you'd better not look."

He smirks, making me doubt him. "I promise," he says.

16

Tensions build with the intense chatter. There are sentries from wall to wall. Alder stands on the platform in front of the frazzled audience, Arcos sits behind him, and little Cy stands at his side. Ruis remains as invisible as always, in the back of the room.

"There have been developments," Alder says, looking over the crowd. "Straif is coming here." A gasp vacuums air from the room. "We must prepare. We must include everyone in the fight." He resists his next statement. "Even our students."

A tall, slender man in a red robe speaks out, "We cannot risk the lives of our young. They are the future of the brethrens."

"There will be no future if the bithling is captured, if Straif is not stopped," Alder says.

Another tall man wearing the same crimson robe shouts from the crowd. "When will he arrive?"

"He's on his way. The celebration is tomorrow. We'll make preparations today."

"May we see the bithling? If we know what it looks like, we'll be better able to protect it," someone in an emerald robe exclaims.

I hold my breath as Alder peers over his men. "There is no need for that. Your only job is to destroy Straif and retrieve the sister key to the Doorway of Feda. My brethren have her in safe keeping."

I'm thankful he does not sell me out. Alder gives instructions, "We will continue with the celebration as planned, however, each of you will need to prepare your brethren. We will assign each group a place to stand guard at all times and the alarm will sound with the first sight of The Thorn. Be armed and have every horse ready for flight. I don't know how or when he will attack, but my suspicions make me believe it will be when the twin moons are at their brightest. That will occur in two nights. We have many civilians here making our task even more complicated. Be prepared my brothers and remember what is at stake."

As the men exit, we head back to our small secluded room. I can't help but think of him. He should be here instead of this "Rowen wanna-a-be." Coll is protecting me for glory, not Rowen. It isn't about him. It's about us. Where is he? Something is wrong. Something is terribly wrong.

The crisp morning light peers in through the window, creeping past my eyelids. The room is hazy and I'm still dazed in a partial state of sleep. Across the room I see him. He's here. His chiseled back moves in perfect motion as I watch him getting dressed. He makes chills move through me like wind over ocean waves. I creep out of my covers and crawl over to the other bed; I slide my hands across his smooth shoulders and press my cheek to his warm skin. "You came back for me." I stay there for a moment his perfection on my cheek.

He turns around. "I never left you."

I jump back in shock. The sun illuminates the miasma of dusty air clouding the room. "It's you! You jerk! You let me...Why didn't you say something? I thought you were..."

"Rowen?" Coll smirks. "I did say something."

"Yeah, but ... you should have said something sooner." My face glows cardinal as I slide back to my side of the room.

"Don't worry, I won't tell anyone."

"Tell anyone what? Nothing happened. I thought you were Rowen, that's all." I stare at his face and see something I have never noticed before. "You know you two look a lot alike."

"That's because he's my twin brother."

"Do what?" I yell. "He's your twin and you aren't the least bit worried about him?"

"My first allegiance is to the brethren. He broke the law. Don't you know what that means?"

"Yeah, it means your law is stupid. He's your own flesh and blood. Your own brother. Aren't you at all worried about him?"

"I won't allow myself." He sits on the edge of the mattress polishing his sword with a cloth, which glimmers against the sunlight, the reflection of his bare chest shining back at him in the blade. "You need to get ready. We have to leave soon."

"You're unbelievable." I jump from the bed.

Entering the bathroom, I notice a sheet is now hanging in the doorway, providing me some privacy. He put the makeshift doorway there—a bit of consideration I didn't think he was capable of. But he still appalls me.

"Hurry up. It's almost time." He works on his blade. Coll does all he can to stay in the frame of mind he was taught to stay in.

After I shower, dress, and come out of the bathroom. Coll is gone. I'm surprised he left me alone. Either something is wrong or something is right. Maybe Rowen has actually come back. With wet hair dripping on the floor, I quietly open the door and peek out. A very large man stands outside with his back to me, his arms folded across his chest. Ruis is beside him. His broad shoulders meet the width of the door. I shut it immediately, tucking myself quietly back into my room. *Okay, now I wouldn't mind having Coll back.* I sit festering.

I hear someone talking loudly and Coll storms in and slams the door. "What's wrong?" I ask.

"He's a traitor! He's turned his back on all of us!" He peers at me with so much anger my soul is scorched. "And he has turned his back on you. Love. It's a joke."

"What are you talking about? Who?"

"We met with Cy, and he had a vision." Anger slices through Coll's words. "Your beloved Rowen, my worthless brother, is with Straif. Cy saw it."

"There has to be some mistake."

"You can live in your make-believe world, Ashe, but it is what it is."

"Exactly, what did he see?"

"Cy's visions are not always specific, but we do know Rowen is with Straif…and that's all I need to know."

"You don't know anything, Coll. You're jealous."

"Jealous?" he laughs. "That he's a traitor? You need to face reality, bithling. He doesn't love you and he never did."

"You're wrong! And don't call me bithling again!" I'm furious. I swelter with anger, leaning my hands on the desk beside my bed. Suddenly, the desk flies across the room, shattering into splinters as it hits the wall. Coll looks at me with disbelief. I don't believe it myself.

The door swings open. "What was that?" Ivy heard the crash from across the hall. She sees the furniture in pieces. "Coll! Wh...what did you do? Ashe, dear, are you hurt?" She scurries toward me placing her arm around my shoulder and giving Coll an evil eye.

"I'm fine. He didn't do it. It just happened."

"What do you mean it just happened?"

"We were arguing and suddenly the desk crashed into the wall."

"She was touching it," Coll adds, which seems unnecessary.

Coll looks at me as if I have the plague. Ivy investigates the destruction. The desk hit the wall, leaving a gaping hole with slivers of wood pierced into the stone. "How did you...?"

"I don't know how it happened." Since I arrived here I've seen stranger things, and a shattered desk isn't the most unbelievable thing I've witnessed.

I'm so worried about Rowen that my mind is still arguing with Coll. "He's wrong. He told me about Rowen. There has to be some mistake. He wouldn't side with Straif. I know he wouldn't."

"Ashe, the truth is Cy saw him. There is no denying that," Ivy reminds me gently.

"We don't know what he saw. And Coll, you said Cy couldn't give you any details."

Both of them wear pity in their eyes, but I refuse to believe Rowen would turn his back on us...on me.

"The celebration is about to begin." Coll's expression is empty, as if he's lost his best friend, but from what I've seen, there was no friendship and no love between them. The fact that they are brothers is still hard for me to get my mind around.

I calm down a bit, but the worry inside me overflows. I know in my heart Rowen would never betray me. Either Cy is lying or something is horribly wrong.

I cover myself in brown, and follow behind Coll while Ivy walks alongside me. As we make our way through the castle's dark and narrow corridor, Ivy explains the purpose of the celebration.

"During the ceremony, the new sentries will receive their rights of passage and take oaths to their assignments."

I hoped this day would be one of joy and I could be one in the crowd. The brown cloak is a safe place and gives me unexpected comfort, but my mind wanders in and out of the thought of Rowen, hoping they are wrong. I know if Rowen is with Straif it isn't of his own free will. I know deep down if what they are saying is true, Rowen is in danger.

As we leave the castle, great masses of people are organized into groups. A rainbow of cloth covers the field of attendants. Each group of brethrens has their own colors. Emerald robes in one group. Crimson in another. Mustard yellow. It's all rather beautiful. We sit in the stands. Only brown robes are amongst us, the youngest of the brethren who are still in training. So, I blend in perfectly. Those who have moved beyond Congramaid, like Coll, Alder, and Ruis, wear no robes, but regular clothes.

My grandfather sits on an ornate wooden throne on the dias alongside the instructors. It doesn't seem like a celebration at all. Even with the thousands of people in attendance, you can hear dust drop and it's creepy. A single instructor stands before the crowd and begins reciting something in a foreign tongue. It sounds like Latin, but I am not really sure.

Not one out of the thousands in the theater utters a sound. The sentries being initiated are motionless in the middle of the theater. The pews are made of stone, much like a Roman Coliseum. I think I'm supposed to be happy for those being placed into the sentry life, but I can't help feeling sorry for them.

The scent of the air changes from a refreshing gust of life to one of foreboding sadness. The atmosphere is thick with solemn darkness, as sinister clouds pull a curtain over the sky. Breathing becomes difficult.

I turn to Coll, who's in some kind of trance. Then I peer over the crowd and everyone is in the same disconnected state. I shake Ivy's sleeve. "What's going on?'

"Shhh. Total silence," she whispers with insistence.

No one seems to recognize the menacing feeling in the air

except for me. The clouds grow darker, but everyone remains dazed. Then, I see him standing at the edge of the crowd, covered in blood.

"Rowen!" I yell at the top of my lungs. Instead of looking at him, the spectators turn their eyes on me and he falters. "Rowen!" I shriek again unconcerned with decorum. My secret is out.

Rowen drops to the ground

Coll looks up and sees his brother, alarm marks his face. He runs toward his brother and I follow right behind him. The entire congregation is in an uproar. All the leaders, including my grandfather, run to Rowen's aid. He's conscious, but barely.

Kneeling by his bruised and broken body, I take his hand and draw it to my chest. "Rowen! Open your eyes. Look at me," I beg him. A strand of black-thorned vine is wrapped around his neck. I try to pull it off, but with each bit of contact the noose tightens more around his throat causing blood to trickle down his muscled neck.

"Don't touch it," Coll instructs, and he gently slips his knife under the vine. With one swift motion, he severs the noose. Rowen groans at the slice and a small glimmer of blue peaks through the small slits of his eyes. Coll picks him up and we make towards the castle. Arcos, Alder, Ruis, Ivy and few of the instructors rush behind us. The celebration stops and everyone is sent back to their quarters. There is no sign of Straif or his thugs.

We end up in one of the dormitory rooms. Coll places Rowen's nearly lifeless body on the bed.

"What happened, my brother?" I'd never seen this side of Coll. His face blushes revealing a bit of compassion. The others stand on the other side of the room except for Alder and Arcos who stay close to Rowen's bedside.

"Str...Straif," the words struggle from his lips. "He was here."

Coll presses his palms on Rowen's chest. After pushing me away, Coll closes his eyes intently. Slowly, the wounds covering Rowen begin to shrink. He's still bleeding, but the red that runs from him slows down. Coll pulls his hands from his brother's chest.

"What are you doing? Why are you stopping?" I ask confused.

"He's a healer; still he can only do so much. Only time will tell," Alder says.

"If you're a healer, why don't you heal him? You're holding

back on purpose? Do something!" I yell in Coll's face. I don't know what he's capable of, and I don't trust him.

Coll is empty and exhausted after sharing his gift. He has no reaction as I scream at him. "What's your problem? Do something!" I continue aggravated with his indifference.

Alder pulls me away from Coll, who now looks like he is on the verge of collapse. "Coll is limited when it comes to healing Rowen."

"I know he is. He hates Rowen. He'd rather see him...." I stop myself before I go too far.

"Let me explain," Alder says as he points to the chair next to Rowen's bed insinuating I take the seat. By this time, Coll is lying down on another bed, looking pathetic and pale.

"Coll is unable to heal himself. The reason he is limited with Rowen is because they are twins. Their DNA is so similar that Coll's gift restricts his ability to help his brother. We'll have to see how effective Coll's powers are on Rowen. He'll have to lay hands upon him several more times, but with each healing Coll gets weaker and has to rest to regain his energy." I can see how the healing affected Coll, who looks like he's run a marathon in one hundred degree temperatures.

"Rowen is going to make it. I know he will," I insist, sitting by his side with his hand in mine. I'm not leaving him. I have him back and I'm not letting him go, not again. My heart aches to see him suffer. Even though I don't like him, I now have a new appreciation for Coll.

Rowen remains unconscious, but the bleeding stops. Coll places hands on his brother's chest ever so often and with each touch Rowen's color improves, his wounds shrink. Each time Coll gives of his gift, he is weaker, like someone recovering from the flu.

Ivy brings us dinner along with my yellow muck. "You need to eat, my dear."

"I'm not leaving his side." She places the food on the floor by my legs. I eat what I can and drink my medicine, which was about half the usual dose. I don't understand what Straif's purpose is in all of this. Why would he want to hurt Rowen? I'm the one he's after, or at least I thought I was. As I gaze down on Rowen's battered face, I realize I'm the reason for his near-death condition. Straif has to be stopped, or I will have to die, yet if I meet my death so will they.

17

The sound of his moaning wakes me from my sleep, his hand still clutched in mine. Arcos has gone to his quarters as did the rest of the crew except for Alder, Coll, and Ruis.

"It's me, Rowen. I'm here."

"Ashe," he groans and touches my cheek bringing with it the warmth I've missed.

"What happened, Rowen?" Alder questions.

"He wants everything. Both keys, Ashe...and the yellow serum. He knows about the serum. He won't quit until he has everything. He thought I had the key. When he found out I didn't ...well, you see what he did. He said this was a warning. He was here, at the celebration. He dropped me in the field behind the dormitories, but I made my way to the ceremony."

"Do you know what his plans are? Did they say anything else you overheard?" Alder asks.

"No, I don't know how they have so much information." His voice is a little stronger now. Apparently, Coll's healing touch made some improvement.

"Did you see anyone who might be giving him inside information?"

Then it hit me like a ton of bricks.

"My art assignment. Bran. He was my art professor at the University of Montana. He had me paint some pictures, and while I was held captive, I saw them hanging on the walls of the caverns. They did something to them. They could see my father and me in the pictures. Like some kind of security system."

"We've got to get those painting...and the sister key," Alders says with worry. "Then we've got to get you out of here and back to Montana."

"I'm not leaving him. I refuse," I spout.

"First things first, Ashe. We've got to get those paintings and find that key."

"I will go," Ruis offers, his face cloaked in trepidation.

"You can't go alone." Alder isn't about to let a rookie take this on.

"I am the only one that's expendable and I have a plan."

Alder shakes his head dismissing the youngster's eagerness and places his hand on Ruis's shoulder in reassurance. "You are not expendable. They'll eat you alive, Ruis."

"I have a plan that will work. They can't know I'm the enemy. They have to think I've turned to their side."

"They will never believe you. It's too risky."

"I'll go to Straif and tell him I've left the brethren. I'll win his trust, find the key and the paintings."

"Ruis, I appreciate your intent." Alder's attitude is saturated with condescension. "Straif is much smarter than that. He'll know." I can tell by Alder's tone he doesn't believe the boy has much wisdom about him.

Suddenly, Ruis's eyes intensify with a metallic glow and he straightens his shoulders. "Watch this," he says. He waves his hand over his face. His clothes turn to black, his nails crusty and yellow. He reeks of rot and decay as his skin darkens, losing its beauty in seconds. He looks exactly like one of The Thorn.

"I don't have much time. I can't stay in this body long or I'll change permanently. My thoughts will become depraved and evil will be engraved in me." He brushes his palm over his face again, returning to his natural state of youth and vigor.

Alder and Rowen look at one another with awestruck expressions. "No one from Congramaid has ever carried this gift. It's only been seen in those of The Thorn," Alder says.

"I've known for a while, Alder. I knew what you would think. It's not something I'm proud of." His expression falls with disappointment.

Alder cannot hide his apprehension, but forces an effort of support. "This is out of your control." He rubs his forehead as if deciphering a complex puzzle.

Rowen falls back to sleep and Coll slumbers on another bed on the other side of the room. Alder and Ruis discuss the plan. They aren't going to tell the others at Congramaid. The less others know about the plan, the better. Ruis is to leave in the evening and infiltrate The Thorn. If they find him out, it'll be the death of him. On the other hand, because his gift is one of evil sorts, they probably won't question his presence. As I listen, I remember the enormity of the Caverns and the masses of artwork that scattered the cave walls. I realize I am the only one who can help. I will have to leave Rowen to save us all.

"I should go with him," I interject.

"I can do this without you," Ruis says. "It's too risky."

"There are thousands of pictures in the caverns. You'll never find my paintings."

"I know what to look for." Ruis seems certain. His secret is out and he's determined to make his mark as part of the brethren.

"Have you been down there? You have no idea how big and confusing that place can be," I explain.

"She's right," Alder says. "If she comes along things will move much faster, limiting the amount of time you'll have to stay in that state, but I'm going with the both of you. We have to get in and out of there fast. Ashe, do you remember how to get to your paintings?"

"Yes, I think I can find them. I remember most of the artwork on the walls of the cave. Unless, they've moved everything, I'll be able to find my way around"

"We'll leave at dawn." Alder and Ruis appear relieved and disappointed at the same time. Ruis will get the opportunity to make his mark. I hope he doesn't lose himself to a world of darkness.

The rain hits the window hard, determined to let me know the skies are gray. I can't tell if dawn made its way through the night.

During the night, someone brought my bag and added three more beds to the room. It is crowded in here, but Alder wants us to remain together. Rowen is looking much better, as is Coll.

I watch him sleep and Rowen's wounds are fading. I am so thankful to have him back. I enjoy watching his body move rhythmically with each breath. I cannot resist the urge to touch him and I move my hand across his forehead.

He is my Montague. I remember the moment he first spoke to me. I was reading Romeo and Juliet. Our relationship has taken on the same ironic twist; our love is forbidden for irrational reasons, and I am determined our ending will be much different. I don't want an ending at all.

I pull myself away from him. Alder and Ruis are gone, so I figure this is a good time to get a shower. The bathroom attached to this room has a door. I'm learning to value little things like privacy now that I'm running around with a bunch of guys. I'm sure if Taylie knew what was going on she would love to switch places with me. She's probably worried sick about me right now.

After my shower, I pull my jeans out of the bag. The stone necklace that was hidden away in my mother's drawer falls out. I trace my finger across the image etched in the stone. Suddenly, images of Nuin surge through my mind as Ivy's gift of memories surfaces. A vivid vision of my mother running toward an enormous oak tree erupts in my brain. Nuin is frantic and has the necklace in her hand. She places it in the knot of the tree and a burst of light emerges. When the vision leaves me, I'm shaking. There's something important about this necklace, something I don't understand. I put it around my neck, to keep from losing it.

I come out of the bathroom and I notice Rowen and Coll's beds are empty. "Rowen? Rowen?" I'm concerned I've uncovered something and I don't know what to do with it.

I open the door leading to the hallway and the same huge guy blocks the entrance, so I tuck myself back into the room and leave the door open behind me. It's weird being alone. I'm usually okay with it, but for some reason solitude is starting to feel uncomfortable.

I hear Alder's voice coming down the corridor, when the bodyguard moves aside and the four brethren walk in. There's obvious distress on their faces.

"We have to find Henry," Rowen demands.

When I hear my father's name, my nerves are zapped again

with worry. "What's wrong with my father?" I ask as fear creeps into my throat.

Alder looks at me reassuringly. "Nothing. He's fine. We are running out of serum and...well, right now we cannot risk bringing your father out into the open, but still, we need more." Rowen sits on the bed with his face in the palms of his hands.

"I know where to find it. But... you're not going to like this. It's in..."

"Stop! Don't tell us where it's hidden!" Coll yells with his hand in the air. "He could be watching us. That's why we left to discuss our plans. Wherever you are," he gestures toward me, "he can see. Remember, your paintings." His distaste for me grows each time he looks at me.

"We'll have no more discussion in your presence. Not until those paintings are destroyed," Alder says. "It's too risky. We're not sure when Straif is watching." Alder is flustered, which is totally out of character for him. Right now, it appears he's losing control.

I'm sick of being in the dark about everything. Seeing my apparent discomfort, Rowen walks over to put his arm around me. His body feels so wonderful up against mine. I stagger from his hand on my back. Coll fumes, irritated by our public display of affection.

"I'm so glad you're better. I was so worried," I say.

"Coll pulled through for me, but it took everything he had."

Rowen looks down and notices the stone hanging from my neck. "Where did you get this?" he asks lifting the pendent from my chest.

"From my mother's dresser at Ivy's house." His eyes gleam as he ogles. "What is it?" I ask.

His hands tremble as he holds the pendent gently in his palm. "This is one of the keys, one of the keys to the doorway of Feda." Alder walks over and his face beams with intrigue.

Excitement surges through me. "We don't have to worry about Straif now. We still have what we need."

"Remember, there are two keys. Straif still has the other one. We'll have to have the other key, as well, in order to have full control of the Doorway of Feda. And the pictures..." Rowen lifts the necklace from around my neck and he puts his forefinger gently over my lips. "Shhhh. You stay here," he whispers as if someone is listening.

For some reason, I still want to keep the key. It was my mother's and I feel closer to her than ever. I want anything that belonged to her.

Moments later, Rowen returns. "Until those pictures are destroyed, you can't have that thing around you. I hope he doesn't already know." If Straif can see me, he can see the key hanging from my neck making me even more his target.

Alder leaves with Ruis, who appears scared and unconfident, to another room to discuss the mission. Coll follows them infuriated by our embrace, slamming the door on his way out.

"I guess he's going to have to get over it," I say.

Rowen peeks into my eyes and kisses me soft and warm, as if he has been holding it in. His lips wrap around mine with perfect design. He was made for me. I can feel it.

After his lips slowly pull away from mine, I see a bit of sadness in the beautiful blue of his eyes.

"What is it?" I ask. His hands still perched around my waist as I surrender to the shape of his fingers.

"Coll will never get over it...but that doesn't really matter now."

I hug him tightly, my cheek pressed up against his chest. "Are they going to let you go?"

"I'm not officially apart of the brethren anymore. I've spoken to Arcos and he knows where I stand and I know where he stands. I'm not leaving you. Not now. Not ever." He smiles with a bit of mischievousness; he has broken the rules and somehow he doesn't care.

"Alder realizes they need me. I may not be of the brethren, but I am still your protector. They will see their options are limited. I won't have it any other way." He leaves me to sit on the bed. "Things are so different now, for me, for you, for Durt."

Because of the spies who watch from a canvas of magical oils, what I'm allowed to know is limited. For now, I'd have to go along with things.

"Ruamna will be here soon."

"I thought only brethren could ride."

"Leprechauns have their ways with horses. Marvin especially.

Lucinda on the other hand, she'll do well by staying on." He smiles. "They're bringing her here."

"Does all this mean we can be together? So, my grandfather approves?"

"He approves of you. He does not approve of us, but that really doesn't matter. Without you nothing else really matters." Taking my hand, he gently pulls me onto the bed and I lay there beside him thankful and worried all at the same time.

"But what about my father?"

"He's safe. We shouldn't discuss that right now. Straif might be watching."

We lay on the bed, my head on his shoulder and his arm around me. It's wonderful being alone with him, without having to please anyone else, without having to abide by some unreasonable law. I could be in love with him, and no one can stop me. No one except for, Straif.

18

Worry clouds the youth on Ruis' face. The fear of who he is about to become takes a toll on him.

"You are going to do great things, Ruis. I know you are." I try to give him support. I try to give him something. I wrap my hand around his forearm and he puts his hand around mine. The moisture of his hand reveals that his nerves are winning.

"How can you have so much faith in me?"

"Because I know deep down inside, you are good, Ruis." I know he isn't fearful of the caverns, but scared of surrendering to darkness, becoming evil for eternity. I feel sorry for him. I really don't know if he'll be able to pull this off or not. I'm not about to let him know I have a bit of doubt.

Rowen's hand touches the back of my arm. "Let's go," he whispers.

Ruis walks away to meet Coll and Alder on the other side of the field. Apparently, we aren't going with them.

"I know you can't tell me what's going on...but what's going on?"

When he looks at me I'm totally vulnerable and totally comfortable. He doesn't have to ask. "Yes, I trust you," I answer.

We stroll toward the stables under cloudy skies. The rain lets up, except for a slight drizzle. Ruamna sees Rowen and neighs, stomping her feet shaking the ground beneath my feet.

"Easy, girl." Marvin brushes down the magnificent sorrel, attempting to keep her calm. Lucinda, on the other hand, sits in a chair a few feet away looking worn and tired. Her hair stands straight on end as if she has been tumbled in a dryer for a couple of hours. I can't help, but chuckle. I guess flying on a giant horse at five thousand feet isn't something that agrees with her. She is oblivious to her disheveled appearance.

"Ashe, dear, you're here. We've been so worried about you." She puts me in the strangulation hold and Marvin joins in.

After they release me from the choke hold, I catch my breath. "How's Dad?"

"He's fine. He's worried about you. We told him we would make sure you're all right. You are all right aren't you?" they ask as if they know something.

"Yes, I'm fine." I don't tell them about the ordeal with Straif. It would make them worry. I'm sure they know what's going on, but I'm not going to give them any details.

They dote over me for a few minutes, while Ruamna and Rowen catch up with one another. Rowen leans his forehead into Ruamna's shoulder breathing her in. The sorrel reaches behind and nudges him on the back with her muzzle, her flaxen mane blends with Rowen's blond hair. One completes the other.

Marvin and Lucinda ask me a thousand questions. It's comforting to see familiar faces. "Tell Dad I love him."

"We will," Lucinda reassures.

With a concerned expression, Marvin leans in and says to Rowen, "I don't know exactly what is going on, but you take care of her, you hear?" He sounds like my father. Well, he sounds like my father would sound if my father was normal.

"I'm not going to let anything happen to her," Rowen answers respectfully.

He jumps onto Ruamna's back and puts his hand out. I take hold without delay. When the horse kneels down, Rowen pulls me up to join him. As we glide into the sky over the field behind Congramaid, I wave 'good-bye' to the Birches, hoping I'll see them again soon.

We fly in the rain for a few minutes, until we break the cloud barrier and we're above the storm. The warm air blows and dries us out. I don't care if I'm wet, cold, or freezing. I'm glad to be with

Rowen. No one flies along with us. It's paradise. I hold on, my arms around him tight, and unrelenting. Every once in a while, he turns and kisses me, without holding back, without anyone watching, without anyone judging.

In the distance, stand the Mountains of Li Sula. Déjà vu visits me with fear as we land in the valley beneath the mountain. Rowen slides off Ruamna's back, and I sit frozen with my hands on her withers. Terror runs through me like sparks of fire. Ruamna is agitated. I hold on to her even tighter.

"Whoa, whoa girl," Rowen tries to calm her.

I can't scream. I can't make a sound. I hold on for dear life when she rears up.

As she stands on her hind legs pawing at the air, my grip loosens and I slide over her rump and off her back. Rowen catches me before I hit the ground. As my touch leaves her, the great horse calms and returns to her normal demeanor.

"What was that all about?" I ask.

"I have no idea." Rowen puts me down gently, my legs shaking. He checks on Ruamna, who is herself again. It was as if a demonic horse spirit momentarily possessed her.

We watch making sure she remains calm, and then we leave her there to graze as we head up the mountainside. I'm uneasy. The walk doesn't seem long, I guess because my mind continues to wander into the world of 'what-ifs.'

Before we proceed through the entry of the caverns, Rowen informs me of the plans. We are to hide out until we have a sign from the others. Ruis is going to transform and approach Straif in his dark form. That will give us time to find the paintings while Alder and Coll hunt for the sister key.

After we sit quietly for a few moments, Rowen notices something. "There," he says pointing. In the sky, are the brethren's horses without riders. We see the silhouette of the massive beasts as they land beside Ruamna. They're apparently glad to see her, neighing and rubbing one another with their muzzles. The peace of watching them has to end. It is time.

We make our way through the entrance. "I'm here," he reassures me. He squeezes my hand gently, and I stop trembling. Even though he is with me, I'm scared to death. The last time I was here, I almost died. This time things are different. I have my protector. I try to convince myself I've nothing to worry about. I take a deep breath and pull myself together. A chill cuts through the air, with the reminder of my last encounter here as the scent of disgust fills my nostrils.

I hear movement in the hallways, but no one appears from behind the sounds. Rowen holds my hand as we make our way down the stairwell, his sword drawn at his side. We hear voices coming toward us, and Rowen pulls me into a small breezeway off to the side of the stairwell. I hold my breath as two dark cloaked The Thorn pass by us preoccupied with chatter. After their passing, we venture further downward deeper into the underground. I start to notice works of art I'd seen during my previous visit.

"I recognize these. We're going the right way," I tell Rowen as he speeds up. He never lets go of my hand. The deeper we delve into the fortress of darkness, the more I recognize and the more terror seeps into the corners of my mind. I wonder if they have anyone else in that cell, or if it was intended for me.

"Turn here." We sneak by the open door to the dining area. It's vacant except for a couple of imps leaning back and dozing in the chairs of the still decorated room. Their obnoxious snores resonate in the hallway as we slip by unnoticed.

"We're getting close. I hope my paintings haven't been moved." I recall the event before I left the cell. Straif tore them from the wall and threw them onto the floor. I doubt they'll still be lying there.

As we approach the room where I had been previously held captive, silence soaks the space with eeriness. My homework isn't on the wall. I look over to the floor where they had been thrown and they are no longer there.

"Great!" I hiss in a whisper. "Now, what do we do?"

"He's probably watching us right now," Rowen points out.

Voices move toward us from the stairwell and one sounds vaguely familiar. I recognize that it's Duir because of the strange hoarseness in his tone. "You can go back. I'll take them to Straif." He sends his help away and calls down from the passageway, "We know you're here."

Rowen pushes me behind him as he shoves our bodies into a small crevice in the wall. Enough space remains for us to breathe as our bodies press together. I could stay here forever, except for the fact that Duir is outside.

"Come out, come out where ever you are," he taunts. "You can't hide forever." He peers around the corner and spots us. He jerks Rowen out first and then me.

"There you are. Now, that wasn't so hard," he says as pride glazes his words. He grabs Rowen by one arm and me by the other. Apparently, he isn't the sharpest tool The Thorn has. In split second, as he occupies both of his hands in our apprehension, Rowen unsheathes his sword and raises it toward Duir. The second rate thug releases me in order to draw his own sword. Suddenly, I'm not scared, but mad. No, make that furious.

As he engages Rowen, in sword-to-sword combat, I don't know what comes over me. I can't sit back and watch. Out of nowhere I reach my hands out and clinch Duir around the waist holding on like a parasite. I don't have a plan, but I'm crazed with anger.

"Get back, Ashe!" Rowen yells at me as Duir tries to pull me off. "Ashe, what do you think you are doing?"

Apparently, I'm not thinking clearly, only reacting. My anger blazes, Duir screams in pain, and his body becomes rigid. He's turning to stone. His waist is hard as rock and the longer I hold on to him, the more he transforms. His screams burse with torment. I jump back, releasing my grip, and the morphing stops short of his face, which remains flesh and blood. His body is stone, complete rock. A gleam of emerald fades from his eyes.

"What have you done to me?" he utters with his last inch of breath. His rocky figure stands in the middle of the room, as his fleshy eyes remain open.

Rowen, walks over to me staring at Duir as he passes by the malformed dead body. "Ashe, how did you do that?" His face is full of shock as he touches Duir's stone arm perplexed by what happened.

I inspect my hands. "I don't know," I say with disbelief. I'm clearly capable of something, but what I don't know. Whatever came over me scares me. *What am I?*

"Come, we must find the others, we must find those paintings." He takes my hand, which I'm not sure he should do at this point. In reflex, I pull my hand out of his. "You won't hurt me. It's okay." I'm hesitant. "I'm still your protector," he says with a sensual smirk.

With apprehension, I give into him and place my hand in his. We race up the stairwell. I have no idea where we are headed. We have no idea where the paintings are, but it's obvious Straif is still watching me. As we move upward, we hear footsteps coming down the stairs toward us. We dart off down an alternate stairwell, headed who knows where. I hear another set of voices. It's Straif. We're getting closer to something.

We find another niche in the wall and scoot into the hidden place while we listen. Straif is close. He's talking to someone whose voice sounds uncomfortably familiar...its Ruis.

"They are here now, my lord," Ruis says. His voice has changed so dramatically that finding young Ruis in the tone is difficult.

"Ruis, what are you doing?" Alder yells.

Our darkest fear has come true. It didn't take long. Ruis has converted over. We've lost him to the darkness. We creep out of our safe place and walk quietly down the steps keeping our backs to the wall. Rowen looks around the corner to see Alder and Coll strapped to the ceiling by chains.

"Ruis, don't do this. Remember. Remember what you are. Remember who you are," Alder pleads. Coll says nothing while fury boils within him. Coll catches a glimpse of Rowen as he stands hidden behind the wall of the stairwell, I hide behind my protector. Alder tries to reason with Ruis. The darkness has destroyed all reason. Alder's voice gets louder and louder, but Ruis is beyond hope.

"Do you think you could do that again?" Rowen murmurs.

"I don't even know what I did," I say. Apparently my whisper wasn't as quiet as his.

"We have visitors," Straif says.

We step out from behind the wall, Rowen with sword drawn. Straif and his new apprentice, Ruis, immediately hold their swords up, ready for combat. Rowen engages the two of them, while I try to free the others, with no success. I hold Alder's chains in my hand and imagine breaking them. Nothing. Nothing at all happens. Okay, if I have some kind of power, I need to know how to use it. When Straif's sword flies through the air and strikes Rowen on the cheek bringing a small bit of red to the surface, rage gushes through me.

Straif hits Rowen with an open hand throwing him across the room, and my wrath unfolds. Something starts to happen, but I don't know what, as the rock above us begins to crumble, Alder's chains fall from the ceiling. Alder looks at me as if he's seen a ghost. Alder swings his sword hitting the shackles wrapping Coll's wrists. They open at the blow and Rowen's twin is released. With his sword Coll does the same for Alder, freeing him from his metal cuffs. All the motion happens in the swiftness of a thought. Rowen is losing the battle and my anger resurfaces. Now, it's three on two: Alder, Rowen and Coll against Ruis and Straif, when two more goons come in to break the odds.

I see my paintings hanging on the wall. As the battle ensues, I take Bran's assignments from the wall and rip them apart as my frustration steams. As I tear, smoke rises from the canvas and soon the paintings turn into flames, I step back as my afflicted artwork burns to ashes. With a demonic look, Ruis grabs me by the wrist and pulls my back up to his chest, facing the others almost as if we are in a violent tango. He has a knife to my throat. This isn't a dance I want to be a part of.

"Now what will you do my brethren?" Venom pours from Ruis's words. My predicament has gotten everyone's attention, and their swords come to a rest at their sides.

"Take your hands off of her," Rowen says.

"Now, why would I do that?" He pauses. "My lord, I have a gift for you."

"Ahhh," Straif sighs. "The brethren has its weaknesses." The words slither across his grey lips.

I place my hands around Ruis's arm, trying to pull away his trembling blade as it teases my throat.

"Don't cut her...we need her alive," Straif reminds him, reaching out his hand toward me, as if I'm a piece of fragile crystal. Ruis is as green now as a Thorn as he was as a sentry. His hands tremble as good and evil battle for his soul. My heart breaks for Ruis as he struggles because I know deep down within him is an innocent boy who is genuinely merciful.

As I hold tight to his forearm, I feel him fighting my relinquishment, when he abruptly lets go. He pushes me away throwing me with all of his strength into the stone wall. I hear the cracking of bone when my arm hits the surface. I agonize in pain and the arm feels broken. It hurts but at least I'm free. Alder, Coll, and Rowen pull their swords and place themselves in front of me. Ruis runs from the room, shamed in front of his new leader.

Straif and his two sidekicks engage what is left of the brethren and Rowen. Alder keeps Straif at bay. Rowen and Coll make mincemeat of the other two which leaves Straif standing alone, his back to the exit. He realizes his predicament and fleas the room, his long black cloak picking up the wind as he speeds away up the stairwell.

Rowen scoops me up and carries me out with Alder and Coll following behind us. My arm is definitely broken. I can't move it and it's disfigured. I support it with my other hand as we rush out.

Now that we'd lost Ruis we'll have to leave without the sister key. The paintings have been destroyed and for now that's as far as we're going to get.

As we run, the pain in my arm is overwhelming, and I bite my lip to keep from screaming. Rowen cradles me in his arms as we rush through the corridors. The roaring of the masses in the distance moves toward us. Alder leads the way and Coll covers us from behind. The crowd gains on us when we get to the exit and a huge man with scraggly blond hair stands at the exit door. He's gigantic, probably seven feet tall and as wide as a mobile home. We aren't going through him, so some way or another we're going to have to take that tree down. Alder goes blade to blade with the giant, when Coll takes his sword and whacks him at the knees bringing him down a couple of feet. We step over him as he bleeds to death without waiting to see what is left.

We sprint toward the valley where the horses wait for us. I brace my right hand around my left forearm to keep it from rattling the fracture.

As we fly over the mountain, Ruis looks up at us as he stands perched on a rock with his black robe fluttering in the false serenity of the wind. His palomino soars the sky alone. We've lost him, and he's lost himself. A feeling of emptiness fills my heart as my hope for him dies.

19

Every time we hit a bump in the wind, pain shoots through me, making me want to pass out. We're headed to Ivy's. "Hang in there," Rowen encourages as he holds me close to his chest. "Whenever we're together, you get hurt. I may not be so good for you after all."

"Don't say that. It's our circumstances. Things won't ever settle down for us. Not until Straif is gone." I strain to speak under the searing pain.

Ivy's house comes into sight and not at all too soon. I dread the landing knowing it's going to hurt. I think Ruamna senses my pain. Her demeanor is much calmer than usual and her landing much smoother than ones I can remember.

Rowen carries me inside. Ivy has returned from Congramaid and she meets us at the door. Arcos along with Cy and a couple of other dignitaries sit in the living room dressed in white robes, except for little Cy who's wearing purple burlap. Rowen lays me on the couch as gently as possible.

"What's wrong?" Arcos asks as he stands.

"Her arm is broken," Coll answers looking me over like livestock. "This is going to hurt."

I'm not at all prepared for what Coll is about to do. "Squeeze my hand," Rowen tells me.

"What ....AHHHHHHHHHH!" I scream at the top of my

lungs. Coll quickly jerks my arm and I hear the crisp sound of bone snapping back into place. This is more than I can handle.

"Sorry, sorry," Rowen recites as he holds my face with his hands trying to get me to focus on something other than my arm.

"Oh, my God! You could have at least warned me!" I scream with tears rolling down my face.

Coll is disconnected. It's as if he's only doing his job. How can someone with such a wonderful gift be so uncaring and cold? The healer continues holding my arm with his hands wrapped firmly around the break. The pain slowly subsides and the swelling is gone a few minutes after Coll releases his grip. I still have some stiffness and soreness but overall it looks as if I've been healed.

"Thanks," I say for lack of words. Coll doesn't respond. He hates me. He only healed me because he had to. If he had his way, I'd be dead and nothing would've happened to his precious brethren, which has dismantled. Only two are left in his group, which is all because of me.

"He really hates me doesn't he?"

"He's confused," Rowen says pulling the stone key from his pocket and putting it around my neck. "I believe this is yours."

"The key!" Cy shouts. "It should not be in her possession."

"It belongs to her," Arcos says.

"But my lord, she doesn't even know what it is, or how to use it."

"Then we will teach her."

"Pardon me, my lord," another of the dignitaries chime in, "but it's much too powerful. It puts all of us at risk."

"She is the only one that has any use for it. And after all, it was her mother's." Argos is firm in his decision.

For a moment, the silence in the room is deafening.

I sit up on the side of the couch, Rowen beside me. Alder gives Arcos, Cy, and the others a run down about what took place in the caverns. "We don't have the sister key and that could present a problem. If Straif locks the door from this side, it will make it impossible for Ashe and Henry to return to the human world."

The conversation soon turns to my sudden abilities in the caverns. "It seems she possesses the gift with the living as well as the nonliving," Alder comments.

"Interesting," Arcos muses.

"She has inherited your gift, Arcos," Ivy says.

My grandfather poses a small grin and a bit of pride makes his face glow. "Her gift goes far beyond mine."

I'm starting to think my gift is invisibility because everyone is talking about me as if I'm not here, so I interject. "Excuse me a second, but can anyone tell me what's going on?"

Arcos has to think about what he's going to say. "Ashe Leigh." He pauses in thought. This is the first time he's called me by name. Actually, no one ever calls me by my full name and it's kind of awkward. "Transference is a rare thing. It can be good or bad. If you and I aren't careful, we can destroy things we cherish along with things we detest."

"Like when I destroyed Duir?"

"You destroyed one of The Thorn?" Alder asks.

"Yes, but I didn't mean to." I thought destroying The Thorn was a good thing, but the expressions on their faces makes me unsure.

Rowen sees my confusion and jumps in. "During our confrontation with Duir, Ashe turned him to stone...well partially."

"When Ruis had you at knife point, what were you thinking?" Alder questions.

"Well, I wanted to get free. I remembered my concern for Ruis and the heartache I felt for him. I wasn't angry, I was empathetic. I wanted him to choose good. I wanted him out of his predicament. I know deep down he is kind-hearted. Really, I care for Ruis and want him back."

"That is why he let her go," Rowen adds as he has a revelation.

"You see, my dear Ashe Leigh, my gift of transference only allows me to affect inanimate objects. My feelings and emotions inflict action only in the nonliving. You, on the other hand, seem to have the power to affect living things as well," my grandfather explains.

"Isn't that dangerous?" I ask, unsure.

"It can be," Cy says. "It can be deadly."

"My lord, would you approve of testing?" one of the dignitaries asks reverently.

My skin crawls. "Testing?" I ask. "What kind of testing? Don't you guys think I've been through enough today? I mean I broke my arm."

Maybe, Arcos is going to care for me as his granddaughter and keep them from using me as a guinea pig. "It is very important we see what you are capable of. Wolfsbane, you may proceed."

Okay, he's going to go through with it. He's going to let them do God knows what. I turn to Rowen. "What are they going to do to me?"

"I'm not sure, but I do know Arcos is not going to let them hurt you," he whispers.

Everyone gets up as we follow the one they called Wolfsbane, outside. He's an awkwardly tall and slender man. I trust Rowen, but I have to admit I'm scared to death. I guess it's not knowing what they're about to do to me or make me do.

Everyone watches as Wolfsbane stands in the middle of a flower garden, closing his eyes and putting out his long slender robe-covered arms. His white hair is wrapped tightly in a bun. He stands there motionless, like a statue. He looks ghostly as his snow white robe glows in the sunlight. Then, suddenly a huge violet and yellow butterfly lands elegantly on his shoulder, then another, and another. They swarm around him in a frenzy. In a few moments, he's covered in butterflies. They are the size of blue jays and every color you could imagine, their wings moving in slow motion keeping them balanced. Wolfsbane's white robe now looks like a moving patchwork quilt as a menagerie of multicolored butterflies envelops him. It's magical.

Wolfsbane looks straight into my eyes. "Come here."

I approach him with uncertainty. He moves slightly and the butterflies flutter off in unison into the wind, except for one which sits quietly in the palm of Wolfsbane's hand.

"Hold out your hand." I do as he instructs. He places the red and white butterfly in my palms, its wings moving up and down to steady its oversized body. "Now, think of something that makes you happy." So, I thought of Rowen. Our first kiss, his hand in the small of my back, him holding me. I remember times with Taylie. When we were young. Growing up together. Slowly, the butterfly glows and shimmers in the sunlight. It lies in my hand as if asleep, tranquil and content.

"Now, think of something that makes you angry, something that infuriates you." That wasn't hard. Straif's vile and distorted face immerges from my mind. I think about my house burning down, about him trying to kill me, about him torturing Rowen. Suddenly, the butterfly grows sharp fangs and spikes emerge from its back, puncturing my hand. Its wings become pointed and its color turns to black and brown. It screeches as if it is in pain. The shrill pierces our ears as the poor creature endures a horrific mutation.

"Enough!" Arcos demands with a regal authoritative tone. Wolfsbane brushes the suffering creature from my hand and it lands on a rose bush, morphing back into its natural state.

Everyone is speechless as we walk back to the house. "How did I do?" I ask Rowen, unsure about what all of this means.

"You did great. Remind me not to cross you off," he says with a grin.

"Don't ever leave me, and you'll be fine," I say, as if I'm okay with what happened. I don't really know what I'm capable of. I don't want to hurt anyone: I don't want to hurt Rowen, or anyone I care about.

Then it all comes back to me, Ruamna's unexpected outburst, the broken desk in the dormitory, and my paintings bursting into flames. I have to be careful. First, my blood is wanted by the darkest of beings and could destroy the universe. Secondly I can kill people by getting angry.

I study my hands. What am I? I want to go back to being simple Ashe Leigh Fair from Darby, Montana. I don't want to be this…this thing. I sit on the couch next to Rowen, hoping I'm not a monster, wishing I could simply be in love like a normal human being. I'm reminded I'm not human when I hear my name.

"Ash-a-Lei-eigh," Wolfsbane speaks my name as if he has a speech impediment. I think he has a hard time saying my name because by doing so he is acknowledging me as a real being and not a bithling. "Now, that you have become of age your powers are being revealed. This is a huge responsibility. You must be aware of your feelings at all times and you must learn to control them. Otherwise, you could hurt the ones you care about as well as those you despise. It'll be a long lesson learned. Be very careful. This isn't something others can teach you. It's something you'll have to learn on your own and unfortunately, at the expense of others."

It would probably be best if I left and hid myself away like a hermit. I'm a danger to everything and everyone around me.

The leaders continue to discuss me and the predicament the world is in. I'm taken aback by all I hear. I'm in my own deep thought as the sound of their voices become indiscernible distant mumbling. I'm not sure what to do with all I've learned about myself.

Coll stands on the other side of the room with his back against the wall and hands slid into the front pockets of his jeans. He stares at me with a smear of abhorrence across his face. I stare back at him. I understood now why he hates me. I can be deadly. I have destroyed his whole world, taken his brother, and now I can destroy him with a single thought and the touch of my hand.

20

The door slams, rattling the windows. "It's gone! It's gone! All of it!" Ivy's voice echoes through the house. I've never heard her demure voice move beyond a loud hush.

At the sound, Rowen jumps from the bed and opens the door. "What's going on?" he asks Alder.

"Don't know." Chaos floods the air.

I rub my eyes trying to wake up. Rowen rushes out of the room. I jump out of bed and run out behind him.

Ivy sits at the kitchen table, her white robe painted with dirt. "It's gone, all of it. I'm supposed to be its keeper…and….it…it's gone." Her demeanor goes from panic to despair.

"Did you check everywhere?" Arcos asks. By now the entire house has come to life and everyone is standing in the kitchen, their faces blank with confusion.

"Everywhere. The entire area." She's out of breath. "They've taken it all. How did they know?" Ivy's crystal eyes pour clear blue drops like a tropical fountain. It's yellow muck, but she acts as if she's lost a loved one.

"Ruis," Coll speaks up. Up until now, he's hardly said a word. "He's told them everything." His brethren is falling apart. I thought I'd lost everything, but in fact Coll is losing his entire world. At least, I've got Rowen. I've taken him from Coll's world into mine.

The window provides a perfect view of the mounds of dirt

cluttering the ground. The once immaculate yard surrounding Ivy's house now looks like a graveyard waiting for freshly assigned corpses. The serum is gone.

"What's Ruis up to?" Rowen asks panning the disrupted view. I take his hand to try to relieve his despair. "What will we do now?" he asks.

"We go back to Montana. I know where there is more muck," I hold up the key.

Rowen towers over the empty holes in the ground. "I don't know if we can go back. Straif has the sister key, which locks the Doorway of Feda from this side. If he's locked it we won't ever be able to go back unless we get his key, plus bringing your father out of hiding would put him at risk too. Straif can never find out he's here, especially now that he knows about the serum. Your father is our only hope for the future."

"Come on," I say pulling him away from the yard and leading him back to the house.

Ivy sits on the couch her face pale and empty. "Aunt Ivy, it's going to be okay," I say kneeling at her feet.

Everyone sits around the room discussing options, while Cy perches in the corner of the room with his eyes closed, apparently trying to see something in his mind. As they ramble on amongst one another without a viable decision, I speak up, "I know where there is more serum." I look back at Rowen for assurance. Everyone stops at my comment.

"Where?" Alder asks.

"In Montana, buried in my yard."

"Impossible. We can't risk it," Coll interjects. I knew he'd be the first one to dismiss anything I said.

"Not impossible," my grandfather says patting Coll on the back. "She does have the key. But returning will be dangerous. And we have to hope Straif has not already locked the door."

"We understand that," Rowen says, "but we have to find more serum and Henry must remain in hiding to work on the formula. It's our only choice."

Cy speaks up from his trance, "If you're going to go then you need to go now. Ruis is headed to the Doorway of Feda. He is going to lock you in. You must go without haste."

"I'm going with you," Coll says staring in my direction. I'm in total disbelief. "I want to make sure you bring my brother back."

"You must go now," Alder urges.

As we head toward the door, Ivy grabs my hand, her porcelain face stained with tracks of tears. "Come back to us, Ashe; I could not bear to lose you, too."

"I will," I say as I hug her tightly. Montana only has a limited supply of muck and it will have to last between the three of us. We'll have to return in order to survive. Hopefully, we'll have enough to last us until Dad can conjure up more. I'm not dead and I have Rowen, so it seems hope is enough…at least for now.

We rush out, mount the horses, and fly toward the Doorway of Feda. I hate leaving my father behind, but I know he's safer in Durt than he'd be back in Montana.

I'm not thrilled about having Coll with us, but I know we need him. His gift is irreplaceable. There is uncertainty of what we are about to face, but I know having Coll can only increase our odds of success.

Rowen pushes Ruamna to her limit, and the horses soar like eagles, the wind blustering against us. On the ground below us, I see black capes flowing on the backs of huge spotted creatures. The Thorn is on the ground headed for the doorway. Instead of horses, the black carpets ride massive cheetahs, their heads twice normal size. Their bodies are muscular and they run at speeds defying the capabilities of any car I've ever seen.

We race them from the sky and at this point we're ahead of them, but only by a small margin. They spot us overhead and force their creatures onward.

Hitting the ground hard on the landing. I almost fall off of Ruamna, but Rowen keeps me astride. We dismount and run for the oak tree. It's the same monstrous tree we portaled through in Rowen's Camaro. Its branches are twisted and tangled, reaching out over an empty meadow as if it owns the land. Its trunk is several feet wide and the bark a smooth rusty brown. There's no time to get Rowen's car. We have to make a run for it.

The Thorn burst through the forest wall with their beasts gnashing and gnarling. With only two or three strides, they are on our heels. Coll runs through first, a burst of golden light beams from the tree on his entry. The Thorn is right behind us. I pause for a moment looking back. Ruis watches me as Rowen pulls me along.

The lost sentry locks eyes to mine. I think I see an ounce of his true self seep through the vapidity of his eyes, but hope will not help him. He's gone and he isn't coming back. He wants my blood as Straif does. He'd drink the elixir of life at my sacrifice and never give it a second thought.

Ruis stands alone with no sign of Straif. The dark leader must have sent Ruis to do his dirty work.

"We've got to move, Ashe, let's go," Rowen says.

As we lunge into the trunk of the tree, a rush of light flashes in front of me. As I float through the portal, I'm in a moment of weightlessness. Then, something grabs hold of my heel. It's a member of The Thorn. I shake my foot and lose him for a split second as we are flushed out of the doorway onto Montana's soil. Rowen pulls the key from my pocket and pushes it through a knot in the tree. Instantly, the bark of the tree begins to change to a glowing brown, surging up through each limb and every leaf. A loud squeal pierces our ears and a hand protrudes from the trunk, turning into wood. The hand looks like a malformed branch and becomes a part of the tree itself.

"That's what happens when the door is locked and someone is still in the doorway. Gotta hurt," Coll says.

I'm breathing heavily. The brothers are also a little out of breath, but not as much as I am.

"We made it," Rowen says.

We walk toward the highway. I'm so glad to be home, to see something familiar.

The sun starts to set and we need to get to the Birches' house as soon as possible. We can figure things out in the morning. Even though my house is gone, I'm home and it feels good.

"So, this is your beloved Montana? Not much to look at." Coll's sarcasm is going to get old.

As we approach the Birches house, Coll's face changes. He blushes a bit. Their home is immaculate and bigger than anything he's seen before, except for Acrimony. He isn't going to admit it, but he's impressed.

I'll sleep better this night alongside Rowen. I know with the door locked from this side, we're safe from The Thorn. Maybe, he could stay with me here in my world, but then I think about it and know without my dad, I can't stay anywhere. Without the yellow muck I'll disappear. I'm unsure of how much muck Dad has buried and I don't know when we'll have to return to Durt, but I'm going to enjoy my time here while it lasts.

When I wake early the next morning, I notice the air doesn't have the same refreshing feeling it usually does and I quickly remember I'm not in Durt anymore. I look to my left and Rowen is sleeping peacefully his face glowing as it did in his homeland. I brush the back of my hand on his cheek and he grins. His eyes still closed, he pulls me closer, and kisses me fully. I want him more each second.

"It's only us here you know?" I say, trying to be seductive, something I'm not skilled at and probably have no business attempting.

"No, we're not alone. Coll is here."

"That's an excuse," I say. "Are you scared of me?" I'm trying to be flirtatious, but I know I'm failing miserably.

"Yes, I am scared," he says.

"Of what?" I'm sure the look on my face spells loser.

"Of what might happen if we did."

"There's no one here, except for Coll. Nothing will happen if we don't want it to." I think I'm starting to sound desperate, but my feelings are overpowering. For the first time I feel we're, well, adults. Alone. No one here to tell us no.

"Did you ever think about what might happen if we had a child?" he asks.

Honestly, until this moment it hadn't crossed my mind. I know I want him and that's all I can think about.

"Our child would be the first...well...the first of its kind. I don't even know what it would be capable of." I have the biggest lump in my gut. This is the worst kind of rejection I could have imagined. He kneels down beside me on the bed, looks deep into my eyes. "I want you more than anything. You have to know that. I'd sacrifice anything for you. I'd sacrifice anything to be with you...except...except our child. I don't want him or her to go through what you have gone through." I know I look pitiful. "We'll work through all of this, but it's going to take time. For now, know I love you."

"I know you do...but...why do you have to be so sensible?"

He chuckles. "You think I'm sensible? The first time I laid

eyes on you I lost all sensibility." And he kisses me softly again. I don't want him to stop…ever.

"Hey, how do you turn the water on in here?" I hear Coll calling from the kitchen. He's lost and I love it, but he stops Rowen in the midst of our ecstasy and I don't appreciate that at all.

"Come. We have a lot to do and a lot to figure out." Rowen takes my hand pulling me away from the bed.

"Hey, somebody show me how to find the water in here?" Coll is flustered. An unfamiliar feeling he doesn't like.

I turn the respective knobs, "hot and cold."

I pull some dried cereal together for breakfast. The milk has gone bad and the bread molded.

After breakfast Rowen tries to crank the Birches old Thunderbird, but it won't start. It's been rebuilt like Rowen's Camaro. "Needs water."

"No problem. I'll get the hose."

"That's not going to help. We have to use water brought here from Durt. The water here has too many contaminants."

I once thought Darby was the purest place in the world. Really, there isn't a place as clean and perfect as Durt.

"We're going to need a car. I can call Taylie."

"Can she keep her mouth shut?" Coll says.

"We're going to have to hope she does. She's the only person around here I trust."

"That doesn't say much." Coll cuts everything I say with a butcher knife.

Rowen jumps in. "You two are going to have to get along if we're going to get anywhere."

"I'm not about to try and meet him half-way. I didn't ask him to come. He volunteered."

"Get hurt again and I bet you won't say that, bithling," Coll sneers.

"Enough! If you don't want to be here, Coll, then go back to Durt. I'll gladly open the door for you! Why did you come?" I've never heard Rowen raise his voice before. "I love her and you're going to have to accept it…or leave."

Coll doesn't say a word. He sits in a state of morose silence when he finally finds words to respond. "Because you are my only brother. Because I don't want to lose you. That's why I'm here."

21

"Taylie?'

"This is Taylie."

I pause for a response, uncertain of what to say. I'm going to shock the crap out of her and that's all there is to it.

"Who is this?"

"Taylie, it's me, Ashe."

"This can't be Ashe. She's dead! Who is this? Why are you calling me?" She becomes hysterical and then I hear a dial tone.

"That didn't go so well. She freaked out and hung up."

"My car may still be at my house. We can walk there if we go through the woods. I can't take the risk of anyone seeing me." We wait for the sun to set before we venture out. We don't use flashlights to limit the risk of being noticed.

The moon glows over every bit of moisture that glazes the forest. I've walked through these woods many times before without a care in the world. I'm always at peace with my surroundings here, a peace that soaks me to the bone, a peace that makes me glad to be in Montana, a peace that makes me glad to be human, when I thought I was human. Now, as I weave in and out of the paths of the trees and brush, I sense the presence of evil following me with blood shot eyes of loathing.

I hold Rowen's hand as we trek through the brush trying to reach my home that's now a pile of rubble. "What is it?" he asks.

"What? I'm fine," I respond attempting to hide my apprehension.

"I can sense a fear building in you."

I stop in my tracks. I jerk away from his grip and look at my hands as if they're some kind of lethal weapon. I realize that whatever I'm feeling can kill him. "I'm sorry, I forgot. I would never forgive myself if I hurt you."

He reaches for my hand and gently puts it back into his. His palm is warm and soft. "You're not going to hurt me. Remember, I have the gift of resistance. We'll have to see how much I can resist."

"It's not worth the risk," I tell him.

"I would risk everything to touch you. I can't live my life without being able to feel. Holding you makes me alive. It reminds me how real we are," he says slowly, gracefully tracing his finger from the soft part of my wrist, down my palm, marking his path to the tip of my finger. A sensual warmth covers me.

I smile. "I love you," I say.

"I know." His eyes glisten along with the dampness of the forest.

"We better catch up with your brother. He looks like he's wandering." Coll is ahead of us and has no idea where he's going. We pick up our pace. "This way," I say as I move ahead still sensitive to a foreboding feeling of evil lurking in the trees.

After about an hour of walking we make it to my house of ashes. My car and Dad's truck are gone. The shed is empty. Nothing's left except for some yellow tape surrounding the area, reading "Crime Scene. Do Not Enter."

I tread through the charred remains of my home and find a picture of my mother scorched around the edges lying underneath some metal sheets that barely survived the blaze. I pick it up, black soot covering my hands. Smoke has taken its toll on the photograph, fading the beautiful eyes that used to graciously look at me.

"What is it?' Rowen asks. I hand him the picture. "Nuin," he says.

I nod.

"Where is the serum?" Coll paces around the yard.

"It should be buried in this area here," I point to the edge of the yard, close to the forest wall. "I'm not sure exactly. I never really paid much attention to where Dad dug," I say thinking I probably should have.

We have nothing to use to dig. "Let's head back to the Birches and we'll try and get Taylie. I don't know what else to do." I agree with Rowen. We don't have any other choice. We have to be as inconspicuous as possible. No one can to know I'm alive. I'm better off dead. At least, it's better for everyone to think I'm dead.

We make it back to the house. I try to think of a way to keep from upsetting Taylie.

As the phone rings, I feel the anticipation of Taylie's reaction. "Taylie, Taylie, don't hang up."

"Who is this?" she says her voice shaking.

"It's me. It's really me, Taylie." There's nothing, but sudden silence. "Taylie? Taylie? Are you there?"

"Ashe....is it really you?" she whispers.

"It's really me. But you can't tell anyone I'm here. You can't say a word to anyone. Not even your parents."

"Where are you?"

"We are at the Birches."

"We? Are you in some kind of trouble?"

"Come over as soon as you can. But Taylie, don't tell anyone."

"I'll be there in a minute."

I know Taylie will keep her word, but I'm worried she might freak when she sees me. There's no easy way to do this.

About thirty minutes later the doorbell rings. I open the door and Taylie gets weak at the knees and all color runs from her face. She's about to go down when Coll comes out of nowhere, catching her, breaking her from the fall.

"You're alive. What happened? Where have you been? And who is this?" she says as she looks up and catches the steel blue of Coll's eyes. She gathers her strength after a brief moment of discombobulating surprise. Coll helps her to her feet, never saying a word. Rowen stands behind me. "What's going on?"

"Sit down, Taylie."

Coll leads her down two steps into the den and then to the couch. Her bewilderment gives her an intoxicated appearance.

"This is Coll, Rowen's twin brother."

Taylie tries to absorb the surrealistic news that I'm alive. I don't think she really understands it all. I don't understand it all.

"Ashe, this is all a bit much."

Coll watches Taylie, almost gawking, never saying a word. I know Taylie is beautiful, but Coll always acts as if he's beyond that, beyond anything human. He's out of character, at least the Coll I know.

Rowen and I explain everything that's happened: Straif, The Dark Thorn, who I am, who my mom was and where she came from. We tell her everything. Taylie sits motionless on the couch trying to reach beyond unbelievability.

"So, what happens now?" she asks.

"We need your help."

"Of course." She doesn't hesitate, even after everything she's heard.

Rowen explains to her that the serum is necessary to keep me alive and he and Coll need it while they're here. "Without it she'll die, well, more like disappear."

"Where's the serum?"

I'm surprised how well Taylie is holding up. She is accepting all of this better than I did, but then again, she isn't being hunted.

"Buried in the backyard at my house."

Taylie starts to giggle. "What's so funny?" I can't believe she's laughing.

"Your dad. He's not so crazy after all."

"No, I guess he isn't," I say as I give her a big hug. She holds on for a minute.

"Don't ever do this to me again," she whispers in my ear squeezing me tighter.

"Never again. I promise."

"Everyone thinks you and your dad are dead and they think he killed you." She points to Rowen.

"Why would they think that? No one here even knows Rowen."

"W...w...well, probably because of me. After your house burned down, I told them he was stalking you, so I gave them his description. They did a sketch. They're looking for him. I'm so sorry. I didn't know. I thought you were dead, too. I thought he killed you." Regret fills the spaces between her words.

"It's alright, Taylie."

"We're going to have to be really careful. We can't be discovered. We need to retrieve the serum, but we'll have to do this at night," Rowen says. "How soon can you take us?"

"Tonight. I'll give my parents some excuse. Don't worry. I'll be here."

Taylie gives me another squeeze as she walks out of the door.

"See you tonight. Thanks so much for helping us," Rowen says standing behind me as we walk Taylie out. Coll stands in the back of the room, silent and out of his element.

"Nice to meet you, Coll," she says peeking around me. He nods awkwardly in response to her subconsciously flirtatious tone.

"See you at sunset."

She picks us up as the sky turns pink and the Montana air develops the sharp edge of a cooler breeze. We take shovels from the Birches' shed and a few empty boxes in which to place the muck along with a couple of flashlights. The ground is still wet from an earlier rain. I have a vague remembrance of Dad digging on the north side of the yard so that's where we start looking. Coll and Rowen move dirt like it's nothing. Even though the ground is soft from a rain days earlier, I make no real difference in the process. Most of the time, I watch Rowen, admiring every piece of him.

I'm a little worried because I haven't had muck for a couple of days and I might start dissipating soon. Coll and Rowen will start to age. We have to find something. As they dig, I see the vapor from the warmth of their breath touching the midnight air with the slightest elegance.

In the midst of it all, I get a strange foreboding someone is watching me. An unsettling feeling, how you would feel when you are about to go into the dentist's office whom doesn't numb you up and you know it's going to hurt. The air is thick. I don't know if the memories of Durt make Darby seem less fresh and wholesome, but something isn't right. My skin tightens as my eyes follow the edge of the yard that meets the national forest. This feeling of discomfort continues to grow. I feel as if my nerves are being removed from my body, one strand at a time, and being knitted into a sweater. I try to focus on finding the muck.

Taylie keeps an eye out as we continue searching. After a couple of hours of digging, Coll hits something in the ground. A jar of muck burst as it meets the shovels edge. "Careful," Rowen says, but beside it are several more jars. We load them up and head back to the Birches. Rowen and Coll are tired. So am I, even though I haven't done much to contribute.

"We'll have to come back tomorrow to find more."

When we get back to our temporary residence, Rowen and Coll bury the muck in the Birches immaculate backyard among all of the flowers and flora that doesn't normally grow in Montana. I guess leprechauns have green thumbs along with red hair. The nights are getting colder and the leaves starting to fall. Still, their yard goes beyond nature.

After our tiring night, Taylie and I go into the kitchen to make popcorn and drinks along with our dose of muck, things Coll has never had. The guys take showers while Taylie and I catch up on things.

"You look different somehow, Ashe."

"Different? I don't look different."

"Yeah, you do. You look happy."

"It's been crazy. One minute I'm living in Montana going to college. The next, I'm fighting for my life in world unlike anything I've ever known. Finding out I'm not who or what I thought I was. And, well, then there's Rowen. He's the best thing that's ever happened to me. He's had to give up everything for me. Everything."

"What do you mean?"

"In Durt, he's held in high esteem. He was chosen at five years old to be my protector, a sentry. They have a vow of celibacy; a vow to never be in a relationship."

"That sucks."

"He's given up everything to be with me. He's been exiled from his brethren."

"His what?"

"His brethren. The group of sentries he was bound to. Now, he really has no home."

"He has you, Ashe."

"I hope he doesn't wake up one day and look at me and realize I'm not worth all of this."

"He never would have given up everything unless he was getting more than he had. He loves you. He chose you. Now, get over it."

It's nice to sit and watch TV. Coll is out of his element. His idea of the human world seems to be changing. Although there's a sharpness in his voice at times, his angry edge has dulled somewhat.

As Rowen and I sit on the couch watching *Casablanca*, Coll sits on one side of the room and Taylie on the other. Awkward. Taylie has never been awkward with guys, never, but Coll is no ordinary guy.

There's still a part of me that's agitated, unsettled.

"What is it?" Rowen asks.

"Nothing. I'm fine."

"Liar," he whispers loud enough for me to hear.

"Okay, I'm not fine. I don't know what it is. Maybe, I'm worried about Dad. Or finding more muck." I don't divulge to him that I thought we were being watched. I don't tell him I was totally creeped out while we were digging.

"We'll find more. We're just getting started. And Henry is exactly where he needs to be. He's doing what has to be done."

"I don't know. I have a feeling something is wrong."

"Stop worrying. Everything is fine." He presses his lips against my forehead and then glues his eyes on Humphrey Bogart. His arm wraps around me like a shawl molded for my body.

It's three in the morning, Taylie has gone home. Coll is asleep in one of the guest rooms, and Rowen is sound asleep. I stare at the ceiling. I can't sleep. A vision of my mother with a tall blond guy keeps resurfacing in my mind. She's holding his hand, as they talk.

"You can't go back," the young man says to her.

"But I have to. I love him."

"You can't love him. He's merely human. Stay here with me and be my wife. There is nothing there for you. You won't survive it. You belong here."

The voices sound so near, and yet, unreachable.

She pushes his hand out of hers gently, but with insistence. "I have to go back to him. I...I...I'm with child."

"You're what?" he yells at her as he steps back. "You're pregnant with a human's child? Do you know what this means?"

"I have to go," she says and she runs from him leaving curtain of despair and worry.

He looks vaguely familiar. I know I've seen him somewhere before. It troubles me that I can't figure it out. Maybe it's a memory given to me by the cube. It all makes me rather uncomfortable. I love the gift Ivy gave me, but sometimes the memories are disturbing. She told me there would be good recollections along with bad. The fact that I don't understand them causes frustration.

I don't want to disturb Rowen so I lift his arm from around my waist and sneak away.

I get a glass of water, something to settle me down. As I stand over the sink filling my glass, I take in a few deep breaths while looking out of the picture window providing a perfect view of the backyard. The moon shines over the lawn, dancing on each dew-covered leaf, embracing them. I remember the times I watched my Dad toiling in our yard with his shovel. Those were peaceful days. I was ignorant to everything then. If I'd only known before what all of his efforts meant. He was trying to protect me. How many people could tell their own child that at age eighteen they would be hunted or vanish? It had to have been so hard for him.

A sudden burst of cold shoots through me when out of the stillness a dark shadow floats across the backyard; a smooth, elegant movement of black that isn't supposed to be there. I put my face up to the glass to see if there's something there or if I'm imagining things.

The warmth of my breath leaves its fog mark on the freezing window pane. Without forewarning Straif's face meets mine. He looks straight at me with an evil, yellow tainted smile filling the pane.

"AHHHHH! Oh my God!" I yell waking the house. Straif is gone in a split second.

"What's wrong?" Rowen is in the kitchen by the time I turn around. My heart beats so hard it hurts and I try to catch my breath.

Coll, rubbing his eyes, follows in right behind him, "What's going on?"

"Str...Stra...Straif. He's here." I can hardly get the words out.

"Impossible," Coll says.

"You're seeing things. Your imagination is getting the best of you," Rowen says placing his hands on my shoulder.

"I'm not seeing things. It's not my imagination. He's here. Why is that impossible? Bran was here when all of this began. Both of you are here. So, Straif could be here too." I'm abashed even though I know what I saw.

Coll wears dubiety. "Straif would never risk himself coming here."

"But the serum was stolen from Ivy's. He probably has it. He has what he needs to be here. We didn't see him riding with The Thorn. So, he must have come through the portal before us." They begin to reconsider their doubt.

"He isn't going to give up on getting Ashe. He wants her more than anything," Rowen adds running his hand through his hair trying to make sense of it all while pacing the floor.

Suddenly, Rowen and Coll look at one another as if they've been discovered with live bombs in their pockets. Rowen bolts out of the back door and Coll is right behind him. I follow. Rowen kneels down and peers into the unearthed graves of muck. "He's taken it." We only had a small supply and we couldn't afford to lose another drop. I'm not losing my mind after all, but now we have bigger problems. He's taken all we'd found.

"He must have slipped in through the portal before us. Ruis stood there watching us walk through the doorway knowing Straif was here." Rowen picks up a handful of fresh loose dirt and watches it fall grain by grain through his fingers.

Coll pats him on the shoulder. "We'll get more tonight."

"And I will guard it with my life," Rowen says.

We go back to bed and I lie there staring at the ceiling. All of this is my fault. Again, everything about who I am hurts everyone I care about. It has been a horrible day. Sometimes I think it would be best if I went to sleep and never woke up.

I turn to Rowen. I study each line of his face, each curve. I realize waking up will be another day with him, and that's something I'll never give up freely.

My mother's memories continue to resurface. I see her standing in a field of lush grass with blades brushing up against her slender calves, the wind touching her hair enough to brush it away from her face, the sun painting her skin with hues of peach and bronze. Standing beside her is the beautiful blond man I'd seen in previous memories, his face still haunting me with familiarity. Déjà vu deluges me. The sun gleams against his skin giving him a rich glow on his smooth complexion. His lips arched slightly at the edge attempting a smile, but something sinister lurks beneath his expression.

As the sun hides behind the distant mountains, Taylie pulls into the driveway. It's time for digging. She brings some of her brother's clothes for Coll and Rowen. They quickly change and we're off again to play in the dirt.

Darkness falls on us quickly. We dig around the edges of our rather large yard a couple of feet into the ground and the sensation comes over me again. Eyes are watching me. I can feel it. I quit my pathetic effort at shoveling and walk toward the forest. A voice in my head calls me, beckoning me.

"I'll be back in a minute," I say.

"Where are you going, Ashe?" Rowen asks.

I don't answer. I keep walking, robotically without my own intention.

"AAshee LLeighh, AAshee LLeighh," the voice calls, the words drawn out in a ghostly tone of endless sound. Nothing around me matters. I only want to follow the voice. "AAshhhe LLeighhh FFFairrrrr," it continues.

"What are you doing?" Rowen has me by both arms shaking me gently.

"What?" I feel as if I've been sleep walking. "Don't you hear it?"

"I don't hear anything." He looks at me as if I've lost my mind. "We're in the middle of nowhere. You took off. Are you alright?"

"I thought I heard someone calling me," I say as I try to figure out what's happened.

"Come back. We've found some more serum. A few more jars. We've got to get back."

Taylie sits on the ground by Coll being her usual loquacious self. The vacant look on Coll's face is priceless.

"Hey guys, while you're all here, there is a concert over at the college tonight. No one will recognize you there. And it'll be dark."

"What is a concert?" Coll asks.

"You're not serious?"

"Taylie, you've got to remember he's not from here. And when I say here, I mean earth." Rowen laughs a little.

Okay, well it's where people sit and listen to music. It's a lot of fun. We ought to go."

"We can't really leave. Someone's got to stay here and watch the muck."

"Coll, you should go with her and get a taste of human life," Rowen adds. "Ashe and I will be fine."

"Alright, I guess I'm in," Coll says. He still has that deer-in-headlights look.

When we arrive back at the house, I'm so glad I'll have Rowen all to myself. The three of us drink our share of muck. There are only a couple of jars left so we are going to have to guard it with our lives.

It's cold outside. We bury the serum, pitch a tent over the mound, and start a fire. We'll have to share a sleeping bag to stay warm. We can only find one. I have to admit I didn't look very hard for a second one. This is going to be the perfect night.

Taylie and Coll come out to the tent before leaving. Taylie looks beautiful as always. Her jeans fit perfectly and her hair is curled to perfection.

"I won't keep him out too long. It's going to be super cold tonight." She takes hold of Coll's hand and pulls him to the car. His lost expression makes him look less like a sentry and more human than he would have wanted to admit.

"Coll has no idea what he's getting into," Rowen chuckles.

"What do you mean?" I pop him on the arm.

"What?" he says innocently. "If he's as lucky as I am, he won't ever look back," and he kisses me long, and as soft as ever as I wrap my arms around him pulling his shirt off from behind. Then I know it's about to happen. Everything about me feels wonderfully different. I give in completely. I don't know what I'm doing and neither does he, but I'm more comfortable than I've ever been. Our breathing is heavy, moving in rhythm as our passion intensifies.

Then ...the phone rings. I brought the cordless outside into the tent and now I wish I hadn't. I try to ignore it.

"Answer it," Rowen says.

"They'll call back."

"Answer it."

Caller ID indicates it's Taylie. "Great. Perfect timing, Taylie."

"Slow down. Taylie, what's wrong!" I can't understand what she's saying behind the hysterics.

For a split second, I wonder what in the world Coll has done. She's crying hysterically. The voice on the phone changes.

"Taylie? Taylie?"

"Let me talk to Rowen." It's Coll.

"What happened? What have you done to her?" I could feel heat building up in my hand and the smell of burning plastic eases into the air.

"Ashe, let me talk to Rowen." His tone is forceful. I hear Taylie screaming in the background. My agitation is about to melt the phone so I hand it over to Rowen.

"Straif," Rowen says.

"What is it?" When Straif's name comes up, the tension in my head begins to mount.

"Are you going there with her?" He pauses. "We'll be here. Take care of her and be safe. Keep us updated on things."

"What is it?" I knew something was terribly wrong when I heard Straif's name.

"There's been an accident. Well, not an accident exactly." I stare at him. "Taylie's house has burnt down. Her entire family." He chokes up, his face falling.

"What? Tell me."

"Taylie's parents, her brother. They're dead. Straif, it has to be at his hand."

"Oh my God! Taylie! I've got to be there for her."

"You can't. It will make things worse, much worse. Coll is with her."

"He hates humans. She needs me, Rowen."

"That's exactly what Straif wants. We have to stay here."

I'm sick to my stomach. Things have gone much too far. We wait in the tent, watching over the muck as we try to keep the fire going. At this point it's all we can do.

We don't hear back from Coll until hours later. They're headed back. The sun creeps through the gold and red tree branches. The evergreens remain brilliant, but I'm no longer a part of this place. I'm disconnected somehow, separated from my true self. I miss Durt and that's something I didn't think I would ever say.

The car pulls in and Coll's driving. He barely misses a tree. I think he's going to give Taylie whiplash. She's a mess. Coll and I help her out of the car. She has makeup smeared down her face. She's still crying, but the tears have dried up. We lead her to the couch. "Taylie, I'm so sorry."

I hold her hands as she sobs and I try to think of the most calming moments in my life. Thoughts of painting and drawing merge through my mind. I envision each stroke and through my transference, Taylie starts to calm down.

"Ashe, I heard the police talking. They're looking for Rowen. They think he's behind all of this."

"I'm gonna move your car to the back of the house to be on the safe side," I say. When I come back inside she's weeping again. I hold her in my arms. "I'm so sorry."

"It has to be Straif," Coll insists.

"I'll kill him. He'll stop at nothing and neither will I." Rowen is beyond anger.

"My aunt is coming down tomorrow to try and plan everything. I can't believe they're really gone." She begins to sob again. "And then I have to get some clothes, something to wear to their funerals."

As I wake up the morning after, I realize the tragedy of yesterday. How I wished it was only a nightmare. Taylie is still asleep. Rowen and Coll are outside guarding our last bit of muck that will only last a couple more days. And I hear the voice again,

"AAshee LLLeighhhh FFFairrrrr, AAshhhhhee LLLeighhhh FFFairrrr." The faint sound drives me crazy as it beckons. Am I losing my mind? Rowen brings in a jar of muck, and I prepare a glass for each of us.

"How's she doing?"

"Better than expected."

"We need to help her out. She's lost everything."

"Come on," Rowen tells me.

We go into the master bedroom. Right behind the dresser is a wall safe. He opens it and pulls out five hundred dollars in twenties. There were several stacks of money remaining. "Tell her to get what she needs." I look at him with confusion. "What?" he asks.

"Where did they get all of this?" Apparently, this is the Birches' stash.

"They're leprechauns. I guess this is their pot of gold."

I hand the money to Taylie. "I can't take this," and she pushes it away.

"Yes, yes, you can. You have to." She looks down at the cash. "Tell Rowen thanks." Reluctantly, she shoves it into her back pocket.

"I want you to go with me."

"You know I can't leave. It's too risky."

"If you change your hair and put on a cap, or something, sunglasses, no one will know you. Ashe, I can't do this by myself."

I told Rowen I'm going with her. "I know she doesn't need to be alone, but we can't risk it," he says as he pours me my daily dose of muck.

"I can't let her be alone, not at a time like this. It's my fault this happened. Straif would have never come here if it weren't for me. Her family is dead because of me." The guilt is overwhelming. I'm losing it as my hands tremble. The glass of muck in my hand shatters cutting my palm. Blood pours out.

"What happened?" Coll rushes in after the glass hits the floor. Rowen wraps my hand up with a towel, but there are still shards of glass in my palm. I shout as he pulls the towel tighter in an attempt to stop the bleeding.

"Ashe wants to go with Taylie, but we can't take the risk of her being seen."

"Where is she going?" Coll questions.

"She's lost everything. Ouch," I mutter as Rowen applies more pressure. Drops of red crimson rain on the floor. "She needs clothes, something to wear to the funeral."

"I'll go with her," Coll volunteers. Rowen and I look at him simultaneously as if something else came out of his mouth.

"Don't be so surprised, Ashe. I'm not as mean as you think I am and besides, no one here knows me. It's the only obvious choice. And she shouldn't be alone at a time like this."

"Stop!" I yell as Rowen continues with his poor attempt at first-aid.

"Here let me handle this. You are so accident prone." Coll places my hand in the sink and turns on the cold water running it over my open bleeding wound. Holding my lacerated hand in the palm of his, slowly, the glass pieces emerged out of the tissue clinking as they fall into the porcelain sink and the open skin begins to close.

As the wound is healed, Taylie comes into the kitchen and sees Rowen wiping up the blood off the floor. "Oh my God. What happened?" Fear and doubt surround her eyes.

"Ashe cut her hand."

She walks over to the sink and inspects my hand. "Where? I don't see a cut." She peers at Coll with apprehension.

"All better now," I say trying to down-play the situation.

"But there's blood everywhere."

"There's something more we haven't told you."

"What?" She trembles as she backs away.

"Calm down. It's not a bad thing."

"Coll. Well, he's a healer."

"A doctor?"

"He's not like one of our doctors. It's a gift." I explain as she walks over to inspect my hand.

"Coll is going to go with you today. It's not safe for me to leave. But you know I would go if I could."

"Are you sure you are up for this?" Taylie asks raising her eyebrows at Coll.

"I'm up for anything. You don't need to be alone. Not now." His tone is without sarcasm.

I am not sure how I'm going to make it happen, but I'm going to be at that funeral.

23

Rowen and I watch the black clad figures from a distance. Coll stands by Taylie at the graveside. I can't believe all he's doing for Taylie, all the support he's giving her. There aren't many people here, a small service at the graveside. Taylie's parents and brother are all buried together. Their remains were burned beyond recognition.

Apparently, Taylie's aunt owns their house and the land. The Winston's lived there and managed the place. As she watches the shovels of dirt cover her brother, Taylie's aunt appears cold and expressionless. It looks like Taylie is on her own.

With her blonde hair blowing in the wind, Taylie sits at the graveside of her family staring at the mound of dirt that covers her past. Coll stands behind her with his hand on her shoulder in consolation.

After everyone is gone, Rowen and I walk over and offer what support we can. Nothing is going to fill the crushing emptiness that soaks Taylie's heart.

No tears. No sobbing. Taylie stands up and looks at me. "Now what?" she says. "I have nothing left and nothing to live for. Tell me what I'm supposed to do now." Her face is flat. Her emotions drained.

"You'll stay with us and we'll figure something out," Rowen says.

I take her hand and head to the gate of the cemetery. Making our way out, I trip over a tombstone falling flat, my hands catching me. Rowen takes my arm helping me up. The marker in front of me catches my eye. I slowly lift my head. The letters N-U-I-N emerge past the bright rays of the sun. Nuin's grave. Iciness overcomes me as I gaze at the tombstone of my mother. She's here. She's actually here. Dad never brought me to the cemetery. I guess coming here made him realize her death all over again. At this moment, I truly feel her death for the first time. Nuin is more real to me now than she ever was.

"Is this the first time you've seen this?" Rowen asks as he puts his arm around me.

"Yes." I stand there and stare at her name for a few moments. As we walk away, a part of me stays behind. Part of me is buried with my mother.

When we get back to the house, everyone is exhausted. I sit back on the couch and take in all that's happened. Taylie falls asleep on the couch across from me.

"I know everyone is tired, but we're going to have to dig tomorrow. We're almost out of serum," Rowen reminds us.

After a few hours of sleep, the voice wakes me. This night the voice is exceptionally strong. It rattles the inside of my head as it pulsates between my ears, pushing against my skull. Apparently, no one else hears it, they're quite asleep. I get up and follow the sound. It leads me outside the house. I push through the darkness, mindless and unaware of direction. I follow the beckoning.

"AAsshheee LLLeighhhh, AAssshhheee LLLeighhhh," it calls. The voice is familiar, but the darkness surrounding it makes it unrecognizable. "AAAssshhheee LLLeighhh." I'm getting closer.

A strong cold wind smacks me in the face and I come out of my stupor. When I come to my senses, I'm standing over the marker of my mother's grave. The voice is gone. I stand in the pitch black, bitter midnight air, barefoot and shivering. The hollow silhouette of the moon hides behind clouds I cannot see. I can feel a presence around me making me unsure of what's about to happen.

"Who's there? Who's there?" I'm terrified, but I try to pretend otherwise. I'm vulnerable, unsure, and at the mercy of the unknown.

I recognize the voice. A voice I hate. "My dear Ashe. You came to see me after all."

"Why did you kill her family? They were no threat to you!

She's no threat to you!" Rage fills me.

"But it was the only way I could get your attention." His voice reeks of evil and is slow and deliberate with each word, taunting and full of malignancy. "If only you would have listened, all of this could have been prevented. What a pity."

I have never been so angry in my life. "Kill me then. And leave everyone else alone."

"Oh, but I plan to." He swaggers toward me with his thin blonde hair and black rob blowing freely behind him. He's standing about twenty feet from me and his putrid scent covers him like maggots. As he moves closer, I turn and run. "You won't get far my dear." His voice reaches beyond the grave on which he stands.

I hide behind the tree line as he crushes the dead leaves on the ground with each step. I try to catch my breath. "I can hear you breathing, Ashe. Don't make this harder than it has to be."

I try to slow my breathing down as I hear his steps ease closer and closer. I run again, but decide to backtrack, returning to Nuin's grave and hiding behind the tombstone. I hope Straif will continue on through the woods, so I crouch down underneath Nuin's name, realizing I may die right where she's buried. I am freezing and I'm concerned the chattering of my teeth will give me away. The footsteps of the evil one approaches when I hear another voice.

"Ashe, Ashe!" I swallow my spit and I want him to stop calling me. "Ashe, Ashe!" Rowen yells.

"What do we have here? Two for one. I couldn't be happier." Straif has Rowen. I remain still keeping quiet. "Ashe Leigh, my dear, you must come and say hello to your sentry, your protector." His tone slithers with repugnance.

"Ashe, stay put," Rowen calls out through a strained voice. I have to do something, anything. "Stay put!" Rowen cries out with effort. I peek around and the moon's glow illuminates the darkness. Straif is much larger than Rowen and not to mention he's armed and Rowen isn't.

I huddle down trying to think of what to do, but I don't have long to figure things out. "Maybe, this will provide you a little encouragement," Straif calls. Whatever he does to Rowen makes him scream out in agony. This is about to stop.

I get up from behind Nuin's name. "Let him go!" I do my best to keep my voice from cracking. He has a knife to Rowen's throat.

"Let him go and I'll go freely."

"Ashe, no. Run!" Rowen shouts and Straif hits him in the face knocking him out cold. He drops him on the ground, unconscious.

"Leave him alone!" I insist. I am boiling with fury, when I realize this might be a good thing. Anger feeds my energy, but I keep control of myself until the right time. Straif walks up to me and grabs me around the neck with his left arm, raising his sword with his right arm.

"I'm taking what is due to me. Don't you see, Ashe? Your mother left me for you, for your father. She took my soul. Now, I'm taking it back."

I wrap my hands around his left arm when he starts to scream. His skin hardens like marble. He drops his sword as the rest of his body becomes petrified. His arm is stone and I feel his chest harden up against my back. His agonizing shriek fades as he becomes a monument towering over my mother's grave with an look of surprise frozen in time. He will spend eternity with her after all. My rage has sculpted its version of evil.

Even though I'm relieved by Straif's destruction, I realize I'm trapped in the statue I've created. Straif's left arm has hardened around my throat. I can barely breathe. I've succeeded in destroying him, but it appears I've also destroyed myself. I strain to cry for help, but I can barely get enough air to breathe much less to talk. Rowen is still lying on the ground, and I'm scared he might be...I can't bring myself to think it. He has to be all right.

I remain here for what seems hours while Rowen lies helpless. The sunrise begins behind the tree line, and I can't wait for the bit of warmth it might offer. Exhaustion takes over from my repeated attempts to escape the stone grip when I hear Rowen groaning. *Thank God. He's alive.*

"Rowen, Rowen," I mutter.

"Ashe, Ashe, Ashe," he mumbles as he slowly comes around. He doesn't hear me. "Ashe, Ashe." Then his eyes find me and the statue of Straif wrapped around my neck. He rushes over and tries to free me from the last bit of wrath left in the evil one.

"Ashe, Ashe!" his voice sounds so far away. Everything is cold. I'm numb. My legs and arms are filled with lead. Time is still. I feel as if I'm separated from my body somehow. Then everything goes black.

24

"She's moving," a voice sounds as if it's coming from the bottom of a well.

"Ashe?"' The voice is clearer now.

My eyes open, but I don't feel I'm moving them with intent. Suddenly the thought of Straif catapults into my mind and I sit straight up.

"Ashe," Rowen says. "Everything is alright. He's dead. You killed him."

We're still in the Darby cemetery. Rowen, Coll and Taylie are all staring down at me. My head is swimming laps. I gather myself and look toward Nuin's grave. There, towering over it is a one armed statue of Straif. His colorless eyes and mouth remain open screaming in silence. It's the most brilliant piece of work I've ever produced.

Relief sets in and I feel finally there'll be rest. Everything will go back to normal, when I realize there's nothing normal about my life. Nothing will ever be normal again.

Rowen helps me up and Taylie gives me a hug. "Let's go h...hom..." She stops herself midsentence with a sadness. I think she realizes she has no real home to go to.

We take it easy the rest of the day until night falls and it's time for muck hunting. We're tired and worn, but there is no time to stop. It's been a tremendous week of shock, a week of sorrow scaring our hearts permanently. We're going to have to return to Durt one day, but I want to stay in Darby for as long as we can. I can't leave Taylie after all she's gone through. She's alone and she needs me. I want to soak in the little bit of calm and peace that has now found its way back into my life. Straif is gone.

We load the shovels in Taylie's car and Rowen drives. I suggest Taylie stay in but she doesn't want to be alone. She sits with Coll in the back seat. They seem a little cozy and I'm taken aback. My imagination is getting away with me. *He's trying to be nice to her. I mean she's lost everything.* I pull myself together and try to stop noticing them. Coll hates humans, and his out-of-character behavior makes me uncomfortable.

I sit with Taylie by the car as the boys turn my yard upside down. They look like a couple of midnight grave diggers. I don't hear any voices tonight, stilling the air with calmness, although the air is only to be still for a moment.

A police car pulls up. He doesn't have his blue lights on. A huge man gets out of his patrol car, inflating his chest making sure we notice his size. Taylie quickly approaches him to keep his eyes away from the rest of us.

"What are you kids doing out here? This place is off limits." His deep voice resonates across the yard. I can barely make out Taylie's stuttering. "We, we....we..." Her nerves are taking over.

"I..I..I'm Taylie Winston. Hangin' out with some friends."

"Wasn't it your house that burned down the other day?"

"Yes, sir," she says as the pitch of her voice turns solemn. She's sinking and I need to rescue her.

"Sorry to hear about that," he says, preoccupied with the rest of us. He takes his beaming spot light and points it at the backyard lighting up the presence of Rowen and Coll. "Hey boys! What are you doing back there?" he yells.

As Taylie's nerves tied her up, I walk toward her as she stands by the police car. "They're friends of ours," I say as if it will help.

"Hold on a minute here," he says giving me the once over with saucer-sized eyes. He looks as if he's won the lottery. "You girls wait right here."

Coll drops his shovel and looks over at us confused. Rowen continues digging, trying to appear innocent. We need that muck.

The officer returns to his car, calling the station and I'm unsure of what he says, but I think I hear my name come up. He steps back out of the car and stares sternly at me. "Yeah, you're that girl. Fair isn't it?"

I keep my mouth shut, not on purpose. I don't know what to say or what to do.

"Yeah, I thought it was you. Why don't you come with me?"

I start to panic as he takes me by the arm escorting me to the car. Rowen heads our way.

"Hey!" he shouts as he sprints across the yard. Coll follows right behind. As Rowen gets closer, the officer gets a look at him.

"And you. Who do we have here? Mr. Arsonist," he mumbles to himself. He shoves me into the backseat and slams the door. He darts toward Rowen.

"I can explain!" I yell hoping my voice is heard through the car window. Then I think about what I've said. I wouldn't really be able to explain anything. Not anything that makes sense. Instead of jail, I'd end up in The Montana Institute for the Mentally Insane.

He seizes Rowen's arm and throws him up against the car pressing his face up against the window. I mouth, "What do I do?"

Taylie makes up as many lies as possible to try and get us out of this predicament. "They're my cousins. They came down for the funeral."

But Barney Fife isn't going to hear it. He's determined to be the local hero. The officer throws a pair of handcuffs on Rowen and shoves him into the back seat next to me.

"Officer! Officer, you've got it all wrong!" Taylie pleads. He ignores her as he calls into the station to inform that he's apprehended the assailant. Taylie begs the police officer. She's crying hysterically." Please! You've got to believe me!" Coll tries to calm her. He's a stranger in another world and confusion shows all over his face. Helpless.

"Miss Winston, if you don't step back and calm down, you will be joining your friends. Now step back!" he commands.

As the police officer continues with his mission, Rowen leans his face a couple of inches away from mine and whispers, "Do you think you could get angry right about now?"

I reach over him, my hands holding the door. I think about being in the back of this car, the death of the Winstons and the death of my mother. Tension burns from my mind through to the tips of my fingers as the car door begins to rattle. The police officer turns to watch his car shaking frantically as if it suffers from seizures.

"What the hell?" he says with his eyes bugging out of his head. The door trembles until its hinges are loosed. Rowen shifts around, his hands still in handcuffs, and kicks the door away. We jump out and head for Taylie's car.

"Come on!" Rowen shouts. Coll and Taylie jump into the back seat and I get behind the wheel.

"We can't go back to the Birches," Rowen says.

The officer trails us. His flashing blue lights immerse the Darby night sky as sirens howl. Taylie's jalopy doesn't have much get up and go, so I do my best to stay ahead.

"Hurry! He's right behind us!" Taylie shouts.

"I don't even know where we're going," I scream panicking.

Rowen is in the passenger seat next to me giving me a look and I know exactly what he wants me to do. We've been through this before.

"Where are we going?" Taylie's voice trembles.

"Durt," Coll responds.

"Do what?" she asks with apprehension.

"You'll be with us," he says. "Everything will be fine." I can't understand how Rowen and Coll can be so calm. I guess it's a part of sentry upbringing.

The tires skid as I head down the old gravel road toward the Doorway of Feda. Everything in front of us is pitch dark and everything behind us is bright blue as the police cars add up one by one. I have no idea what's ahead and the abilities of Taylie's car are limited. The dirt road permeates the air with a dust cloud trailing behind us. Then I notice the gas gauge is set on E.

"We're almost out of gas."

"Turn off the lights," Rowen says. I know sentries have a 'no-worry' kind of attitude, but this is ridiculous. I can't see in front of me and I everything I see behind us isn't good. Not good at all.

"I can't see with them off, Rowen! I'm having a hard enough time driving this thing as it is!"

"Move over."

"Move over where? And what are you going to do with your hands still in cuffs!" Rowen reaches over me and switches off the lights. With a jolt, one of the cop cars rams us and I struggle to keep the car on the road. I keep one hand on the wheel and the other on Rowen's handcuffs. My agitation transfers through the metal dropping them from his wrists.

Rowen takes hold of the steering wheel. "Keep your foot on the gas, floor it."

He sits in my lap steering the car. I pull my foot off the gas pedal and he takes over. I crawl over to the passenger seat holding on for dear life.

Rowen is able to push the car further and drives into the blackness for a few minutes. The only thing I can see are blue lights in the distance behind us. The car begins to sputter as the motor hangs on to the last bit of fumes. Rowen rolls the car into a field of tall, thick brush.

"Come on," Rowen says as I crawl out behind him through the driver's door. He leads us through the eight feet tall vegetation. Taylie and Coll are right behind us as we move quickly and quietly away from the car, with no idea where we are or where we're headed. Seeing beyond the brush is impossible.

We only see the occasional break of beaming lights and hear barking dogs in the distance. They're getting closer to us and we have to find a way out of this endless maze. Finally, we come to a clearing and there it is at the end of the road, the Great Oak. Sapphire light beams move across the night sky and frantic voices resonate.

As we approach the tree, I pull the key from around my neck and hand it to Rowen.

"Hold it!" a cop shouts as a ray of blinding light hits us directly in the face. Rowen slips the key into the portal unlocking our escape. Grasping my hand, Rowen steps through the portal door pulling me along. I turn and take hold of Taylie bringing her with me. My eye catches Coll as he's apprehended, and he gives the officer a right hook. There's no turning back. The three of us move through the portal and Coll is on his own.

25

I'm in a moment of weightlessness as we're transported. Then, I feel the ground support me once again. Taylie looks dazed. We're relieved Ruis left the portal unlocked awaiting Straif's return.

The night sky glows with a magnificent pink hue as the lavender moons shimmer above us, reminding me where I am. Rowen searches the area to make sure we're alone. There's no sign of The Thorn, at least not now.

"It's okay, Taylie. Everything's okay," I try to reassure her. She looks around as if she's lost.

Rowen watches the tree for any sign of his brother. "I'm going back for him," Rowen says.

"Give him a few more minutes," I plead knowing deep down Rowen isn't going to leave his brother behind and I know he shouldn't. The thought of being alone at night in Durt is unsettling. What if he doesn't come back?

"Ashe, you know I can't leave him there."

"I know." I hold on to him for a moment, letting him go with trepidation. Approaching the doorway, the bark glows a brilliant gold with light enveloping the tree. Rowen stops as a figure protrudes beyond the light. Coll steps through the Doorway of Feda. He's made it, but a little worse for wear. His clothes are disheveled and he has a rather brilliant black eye.

"I was coming back for you. What took you so long?" Rowen

says grabbing his brother up into a big bear hug.

"The other guy looks much worse. I think I knocked him out. I wanted to make sure he didn't try and follow us."

I'm not sure, but I thought Coll gave Taylie a weird look and not an ordinary Coll expression. Then I remember how he hates humans, how he hates anyone who isn't his kind.

We head to Ivy's house. It's dark. There are sounds in the woods of this land I haven't heard before. Sounds that are peaceful and sedating and others that will make your skin crawl. I hold on to Rowen and think about getting somewhere quiet, somewhere safe. It's comforting to know, however, Straif is gone and I can relax on that account.

Taylie, on the other hand, isn't saying much. Actually, she isn't saying anything and that isn't like her at all. I know she has to be in shock. I've been through the same thing once before. I check with her every once in a while, reassuring her we're with the protectors who'll do just that. She only nods. I don't like the fear I see in her eyes. I feel deeply for her, but really, there's nothing I can do to make things better. Only time has the power to give her comfort now. I'm going to be here for her because now it appears we'll never go back to Montana.

We're exhausted. Right now, I only want to get somewhere to rest. So, when I see Ivy's house I'm elated. "Thank God we're here!" I shout.

"Shhhh." Coll says. "You'll alarm Ms. Ivy. She won't be expecting us."

"Who's Ivy?" Taylie ask. That's the first thing I've heard her say since we arrived.

"Oh, sorry Taylie. She's my great aunt. My grandmother's sister."

As we approach the house we notice the extreme darkness surrounding it. As we get closer, we see the front door lying on the ground.

"Stay here," Rowen says as he gently pushes me away from the house.

We wait outside for a few minutes and I then my patience gets the best of me and I follow in after him.

"He said to wait here," Coll blurts with derision. I ignore him. The house is in shambles. Broken bits of furniture lay formless on the floor. Windows are busted out.

"Rowen," I call out. The house is abandoned. I hope Ivy is in safe-keeping.

"What are you doing in here?" Rowen asks without surprise as he walks into what was once a beautiful living room.

"What happened?"

"I don't know, but I have an idea. I can't bring myself to say it."

"Ruis," Coll says as he steps through the dismantled doorway. Taylie walks in behind him.

"We'll have to stay here tonight and decide what to do in the morning," Rowen says. "Tomorrow you'll need serum. I'm not letting you go days without it again. It's too risky. I hope Henry has succeeded with the serum by now."

Rowen and I stay in Nuin's room, while Taylie and Coll find beds that haven't been totally destroyed. Right when I think things are looking up, my hopes vaporize.

I thought this would have been a sleepless night, but turns out I slept better than I have in a long time. No dreams, no voices. The silence is tranquilizing.

The beautiful sun beams through the stained glass window, waking me up at dawn. Rowen sleeps soundly and the house is quiet except for the angelic voices of birds outside the busted window. I imagine the trauma and torment causing the broken pane and my heart sinks as I began to worry about Ivy and Dad. We have to get to Acrimony, but I don't know how that's going to happen.

Quietly, I go to the kitchen and sit at the table, worried and confused. I know Rowen will take care of it. But this is his world and I'm not sure where I belong. I'm more confused now than I've ever been in my life. I sit here with my face in my hands, and then I feel the warmth of his lips on the back of my neck sending electric fire through my body. He releases his touch and takes the seat opposite me.

"You all right?" he asks as he bites into an apple that's fallen from the fruit bowl.

"Worried about Ivy, Dad ....everything."

"We have to get to the castle," he says taking another bite.

"Do you have any suggestions?" I ask.

"Coll and I will figure something out." He's always so calm

and collected which helps me worry less.

"Did you hear that?" he asks as he stops chewing.

"Hear what?"

"Shhhh." I listen intently without hearing a sound. "Listen. There it is again," he whispers.

Rowen jumps from the chair and runs outside. I chase after him."Ruamna!" he yells as he heads to the field of knee high brilliant green grass. Butterflies fly amongst the blooms painting the horizon. "Ruamna!"

Coll comes running out. "What's going on?"

"Listen," Rowen says.

Coll's eyes grow big. "I hear them. Mugwort!" he calls.

"Who is Mugwort?"

"His black stallion," Rowen says in a lower tone that isn't quite a whisper.

As we stand in the middle of this beautiful meadow, I hear a whinny. Then the ground starts to tremble as two horses burst through the forest wall heading straight for us. I stand behind Rowen, worried they won't stop. The stampede ends short of us, as Ruamna and Mugwort walk up. The brothers are so glad to see them, rubbing their faces into the shoulders of the massive equines.

"I guess we have our way to Acrimony."

"Yes, we sure do." Rowen smiles.

We walk back to the house, the horses following behind. Taylie stands in the doorway.

"What in the world?" she says. Her look of shock is probably no different than mine the day I was greeted by four of the same magnificent creatures.

"Don't be worried. They're our flight to the Castle of Acrimony," I say.

"Acri...what?"

"It's where my grandfather lives. We'll be safer and more comfortable there," I say hoping I'm telling her the truth.

26

We clean ourselves up and pack what's left of Nuin's personal things. Taylie still isn't saying much. Her life has been turned upside down and I'm to blame. At least I still have my father and I have Rowen. She's lost her family, her home, her entire life. I'm going to do whatever I can to make her time here the best it can be. In grade school, there were many times Taylie took up for me. It's my turn to take care of her.

Rowen and Coll are waiting for us outside. "Ready?" I ask her.

"I don't know."

"Everything will be fine. You'll see."

As we walk out and I can tell Taylie is terrified although she tries to hide it.

Rowen sits on Ruamna. I take his hand and he pulls me up as if it's nothing.

"Give me your hand," Coll says. Taylie is hesitant.

She approaches with caution, as Mugwort gushes air through his nostrils. "Don't be afraid. He won't hurt you," Coll says. She offers her hand and he lifts her swiftly. She holds onto him for dear life. I'm worried because she doesn't know it, but she hasn't seen anything yet. *Wait until we are in the air.*

We run through the meadow for a few strides, then the horses leave the ground. Their wings fill the sky.

"Hang on," I yell. Taylie's eyes close tightly and then she

buries her face into Coll's back. She remains this way for quite a while then slowly opens her eyes and squeaks a peek. Me, on the other hand, this has become my perfect delight. I've finally overcome the rollercoaster.

Acrimony comes into view. It's as beautiful and inviting as usual. I recall the tension during our last visit. I hope Arcos sees things differently now that Straif is dead.

We land by the stables. Marvin and Lucinda are waiting for us. How they knew we were coming, I have no idea. As soon as we hit the ground, both of them come running. The boys dismount and help Taylie and me to the ground. Lucinda hugs me as soon as her arms can reach me. Marvin shakes both of the boys' arms.

"How did you know to send Ruamna and Mugwort?" Rowen asks.

"I knew when you returned Ivy's would be the first place you would go. So, I sent them there." Marvin explains.

"Exactly, what happened?" Coll asks.

"Ruis. He's gone mad. He dismantled Ivy's cottage looking for the muck, looking for anything. He's crazed for power."

"Are Ivy and Dad okay?" I ask.

"Yes, dear, they're both fine. Ivy escaped to the woods where she was found later and your Dad is still safe in hiding, under the highest protection. I see Ashe's young friend has traveled with you," he comments raising his bushy red eyebrows that look like giant red caterpillars.

"I can explain. We have great news and not so great news," Rowen adds as we follow the Birches to the castle.

"Let's wait until we meet with His Majesty. He'll want to be the first to hear," Marvin suggests.

I wrap arms with Taylie and walk with her. She's still overwhelmed. "Don't be afraid. It's my grandfather."

"I'm not afraid. I miss my family," she says solemnly.

After entering, we're lead to a grand sitting room with large plump sofas and oversized chairs. The atmosphere is much more welcoming than the last time I was here. Taylie and I plop down on one of the sofas while Coll and Rowen recline in armchairs. We gaze at the enormity of the room. I marvel at the exquisite Baroque style paintings scaling the walls. This room has a home-like presence, but on a bigger scale. We sit quietly for a minute when the door opens and I cannot believe my eyes.

"Dad!" I haven't seen him in what seems forever. Two large men follow behind him. I dart to him realizing how much I missed him.

"Ashe," he says holding me tight. "We have serum." He's proud. I should have known that would be the first thing out of his mouth.

"Good, because I'm due a dose."

"How long has it been?" he says with obvious concern.

"A couple of days," I answer. He shoots out of the room, his mind redirecting him with the two body guards chasing behind him. Arcos and his entourage meander around him and make their way through the door. Rowen and Coll jump from their chairs to a standing position and bow at the waist.

"Sit," Arcos instructs and we all take our seats. He turns to Rowen looking at him as if to say what have you done now, but instead he asks, "Who have you brought with you?"

"This is Taylie. She's Ashe's closest friend."

"Hello, Taylie," Arcos greets. "What brings you to Durt?"

Taylie looks at me, at a loss for words. "Straif. He killed her family. Her entire family." Arcos's face goes beyond the pale he usually wears. "She had to come with us. We...we..." I stutter unsure of what I'm supposed to say. She's human, but I guess that's a step up from being a bithling.

Arcos puts his hand up in the air to silence me. I shut my mouth rather quickly to keep from saying anything that might make things more awkward." I'm so sorry for you, Taylie. You are welcome here." He turns to Rowen whom quickly shares the events of Montana.

"So, Ashe, you were able to control your powers enough to destroy Straif? I'm very proud of you. It appears you are succeeding with self-control."

I feel relieved that he's beginning to accept me.

"There have been disturbing events here as well." He rubs his hands together slowly. "Ruis."

I began to feel sick to my stomach.

"Ruis," Arcos continues. "He's gone mad, running reckless across the land of Acrimony, threatening the stability of Congramaid. He's even terrorized the village of Skewantee, killing and maiming." My mind immediately goes to Scout and his family. First Straif, now Ruis. Is this insanity ever going to end?

Arcos stands, stroking his long braided beard. "We need to reassemble what is left of the brethren. We need every force, every sentry available. Alder is on his way back from Congramaid and will discuss with you plans needed to protect our future." Arcos leaves the room his group surrounding him.

"What's wrong now?" Taylie asks. I feel so sorry for her. She's been thrown into this entirely new existence without a clue about what is going on. She's never been this closed up and quiet. I hate we've taken her joy. We've taken everything from her. All I really want to do is help her find the part of her that used to make her glow, that part that made her Taylie.

The door burst open and Dad has a glass full of muck. "Here, drink up." I do as he says and I'm glad to have my medicine again. "We have plenty now. Don't forget to take it. Do you understand?"

I hug him. "I love you, Dad."

He doesn't know what to do with the affection. Awkwardly, he hugs me back. "Don't forget," he says adamantly and he lightly kisses my forehead.

"I won't."

"I've got to get back to work," and he darts away.

We're escorted to separate rooms. Rowen and Coll are down the hall from Taylie and me. She's in an immaculate space covered in white linens right next door to me. The moon beams through the stained glass window lighting the room with gold and green hues.

"Are you going to be okay?" I ask.

"I'm feeling so empty, so lost," she says. Her voice is vacant, without life.

"It's going to take time."

"I know, Ashe."

"I'll be next door if you need anything, anything at all." I go to my room which is as beautiful as Taylie's. A huge bed stands three feet off the floor with lush pink and yellow pillows.

I want Rowen with me, but I know while we're in Acrimony we'll have to be discreet. Arcos has apparently accepted Rowen back into the brethren and I'm not going to do anything to agitate the situation.

I think of the loneliness swallowing Taylie's heart. I'm

thankful for what I have. Thankful for all the crazy things that have become a part of my life and I'm not going to take anything for granted, not ever again.

I wake the next morning to Rowen's soft sweet kiss. He leans over me as I wake. "Alder will be here soon. I'll come and find you when we're through."

"You'd better not be all day," I say jokingly. He gives me a look reeling me in, closing the door behind him. Things have calmed down in Durt, but I don't know how long this period will last. Rowen and I are together, Dad is safe and he's here, Arcos has accepted us; well, maybe not completely, but he's more accepting than he has been. I know he only let Rowen back into the Order of the Brethren out of necessity, for the safety of Durt, but reason doesn't matter. We're together making me feel complete. But I feel guilty for the bit of contentment I have. Taylie's world has been destroyed.

We have a bit of breakfast and spend most of the morning roaming the grounds. Taylie and I take in all the beauty of Acrimony. "So, what does one do here?" she asks.

"Well, my time here has been one of survival. I really haven't had a chance to enjoy any of this."

Rowen and Coll meet up with us later in the day. We walk through the forest encircling the castle. The trees are greener than green. Vibrant. Flowers bloom in every patch of meadow. I don't think I've ever been happier than I am at this very moment.

We find a waterfall tumbling hundreds of feet into a pool of clear aqua blue. We swim in our clothes and lay in the amber sun until we dry off. I wish everyday could be like this. Taylie is even able to break a smile here and there. It's exactly what she needed. It's what we all needed.

"Are you getting used to Durt now?" Rowen asks as we lay on the warm rocks, soaking up the warmth of the sky.

"I could get used to this, but it doesn't really matter where we are, as long as we are together." He smiles, looking down into my eyes and brushing the wet hair from my face.

"We need to head back." He stands reaching down for my hand then pulling me up. I'm about to let go of his tender grip when he brings me up close to his bare chest, kissing me softly. Yeah, I could get used to this.

It appears Coll has made an exception for humans now that he's met Taylie. Bithlings on the other hand, are still not on his list of favorite things. I've seen them strolling through the gardens, sitting next to one another during meals and sometimes there both gone at the same time with no explanation.

I haven't seen much of Arcos either. I wander around the castle on my own feeding my curiosity by looking into rooms and meandering through corridors. It's a building of endless size. It goes on forever. I get lost finding my way back to my room when I stumble into a small room that's apparently an artist's studio, filled with canvases, sculptures, easels, and brushes. Dust covers every inch of the space, wooden bowls filled with dried paint and bristles of brushes dried up and broken. A stool sits in front of an easel holding a canvas of unfinished work. I ease onto the painter's stool, and study the painting. The emerging subject has a very strong resemblance to my father. I trace my finger over the curved lines of dried, old paint.

"I see your mother when I look at you." I jump out of my skin and almost fall to the floor. Arcos is standing in the doorway.

"I'm sorry...I...I .... I'm taking look around."

"No harm. All is well, my dear." He strolls into the room gently running his hands over his braided beard. His white robe flows behind him like angel's wings. He towers over me as he peers over my shoulder at the unfinished artwork.

"So, who's the artist?"

"This was Nuin's favorite place. Here in Durt we cherish those creative abilities. It is a gift not everyone holds. It is a gift treasured beyond the gift of living. For it is through these creative gifts life is captured for eternity."

A feeling of warmth covers me like lamb's wool when I realize I'm sitting in my mother's studio.

"This was going to be a portrait of my father," I say staring at the canvas with tears whelping up in my eyes. "She didn't get to finish it."

"No, but you may want to finish it for her," he says. "You can come here anytime you like. Use this room at your leisure. I think Nuin would love to have given this room to you herself." Looking at me over his shoulder, he walks out.

Quietly, I cry. I feel her here. I miss her. I long for her. Now, I'm able to admit it, at least to myself.

During dinner, things are quiet. There's no talk of Ruis, The Dark Thorn or any plans of attack. Things are calm and I'm glad. It's time for peace, time to stop running after or away.

Taylie and I head back to our rooms after dinner. A twinkle of her old glow is coming back. But there's still an unhappiness blocking her from fully experiencing the beauty of Durt.

"I miss them so much," she says.

"I know it has to be hard. I'm sorry this happened to you and it's all because of me, because of what I am."

"This isn't your fault, Ashe. I don't blame you. I only blame the one who did it and he's dead." She walks with me down the last corridor, locking arms with mine. "At least we have each other. I believe things will get better with time. They have to."

She hugs me tight and then goes to her room.

The stained glass windows of my room open onto a balcony. I take in a big breath of fresh air. I'm so high above the ground, I can see the tops of the trees. The stars light the sky like fireworks. He sneaks behind gently wrapping his fingers around my waist, saying nothing. I enjoy his touch, my hands on the rails as I absorb the serenity around us.

"Things are quiet," I say listening to the solitude of the woods.

"They seem so." His manner is doubtful.

"What is it? Is something wrong?"

"Ruis isn't going to stay quiet. He has to know Straif is gone. The power is his now if he wants it. I believe he does want it. He has to be up to something."

"Ruis isn't truly wicked. Deep within his soul, there is good. He did let me go you know."

"He had no other choice." Rowen releases his caress and stands beside me looking out. "I believe he encouraged Straif to go to Montana, because he knows what you are capable of. He knew Straif would not be able to defeat you. Ruis was not able to resist your transference and he knew Straif wouldn't either." He pauses. "And now he is free to rule."

"I don't think Ruis is like that."

"Ashe, Ruis has the gift of deception. His entire body is programmed for evil, for destruction. It's who he is now."

"I don't believe it."

He kisses me quickly on the lips. "Go to sleep. You're tired."

"Good night." I wanted to be able to say good morning instead. He makes me feel complete.

"Good night," he whispers as he holds me for a moment under the starlight.

Taylie didn't make it down to breakfast and no one has seen her.

"Taylie, wake up." I knock on her door, but she doesn't answer. I let myself in. "Taylie, Taylie." Her bed is empty. Where is she?

I find Rowen and Coll and we search everywhere for her, the gardens, the castle, the stable, everywhere. There's no sign of her.

"I hope she hasn't done something crazy."

"She wouldn't do that," Coll says defensively.

"I'm not saying she would do it on purpose, Coll. You don't even know her," I spout back. Who does he think he is? He hardly knows her.

"We have to find her," Rowen says. "Ashe, did you see anything in her room that would make you think she left? Maybe, she tried to go back to Montana."

We go back to her room to see if we can find a clue, anything that will give us answers.

"Nothing," Coll says.

I plop onto the bed and something sharp pokes me through the covers.

"Ouch!" I yell, jumping up and pulling back the sheets. An iridescent black ring of thorns is buried under the bedding. I look at Rowen for an answer.

"He's taken her," he says.

"Why?" I yell. "Why would he want her?"

"He's trying get to you. Come, we've got to find Alder."

We go to Ivy's room on the ground floor. "Ashe, you stay here with Ivy. We will place a guard at your door."

"What? I'm going with you!"

"That's exactly what Ruis wants. If you want to help, you'll stay here." Rowen is ordering me to stay as he holds his hand firmly against my shoulder. He's never spoken to me this way before. My heart sinks to the floor. Before he exits, he looks at me as if he's in pain. I drop in the chair, vacant and confused.

"It is for the best, Ashe. They have to find Taylie. If you went along you would be a distraction. He'd be trying to protect you as well as Taylie. You understand. Don't you?" Ivy asks.

"I don't understand anything."

I slouch in the chair for hours, staring out of the window until night falls and she is asleep. It's now or never.

27

The night sky is over cast. The moon is not as bright as I would have liked, but I can't let that stop me. Ivy doesn't even notice as I slip out of the window. I can't believe what I'm about to do.

The stables are abandoned of anyone except for the horses. It's quiet except for sound of munching on hay and a few snorts here and there.

I ease open the stall door and my grandfather's horse looks me straight in the eyes stomping his massive hooves impatiently into the ground.

He's majestic and intimidating. I'm scared to death and I think he knows it. I have no idea if he'll accept me or even understand me, but I have to take the chance. He's royalty when it comes to horses and I'm supposed to be royalty, too. So, hopefully that will account for something.

"Easy, easy," I say as if it'll make a difference. How the hell am I supposed to get on this thing? I'll need a ladder to reach his shoulders. He rears up spreading his enormous wings, hitting me in the chest and knocking me to the ground. After he knocks the breath out of me, it takes me a minute to re-inflate my lungs. I pull myself together and get back up.

"I don't know how, but we're going to do this," I say. I'm about to approach him again and hear a deep familiar voice.

"Whoa." It's Marvin. The great white animal is motionless at the sound of his voice.

"How did you think you were going to get on his back?"

"I didn't know and still don't know. I'm kind of figuring this out as I go." Marvin leads him from the stall.

"Sleuchd," Marvin says firmly and the white horse kneels down on both knees. "Dagda is all yours."

I'm a nervous wreck. I have to get a hold of myself. Any agitation I have will transfer into the horse, making this a rough ride. Taking a deep breath I tell myself I can do this. I was born to do this. I'm the protector now.

I take hold of his thick, snow-white mane and pull myself onto his back. When he stands up on all fours, I'm so high off the ground my stomach starts to turn. Get a grip. Remain calm. This ride is already a risky one.

"What do I do now?" I ask Marvin as Dagda stomps his feet.

"Think about where you want to go and he'll know."

"Aren't you are going to try and stop me?"

"Ashe, when I look at you I see your mother. There's so much about you that is like her. She was free-spirited and independent. That is you. It's always been you. You didn't know it until you were forced to become whom you were meant to be."

"I'm not sure if I can do this, Marvin, but I've got to try." He hits Dagda on his scaled flank. The horse takes off in a gallop then hits the sky as I picture the Mountains of Li Sula.

The air becomes warmer the higher we fly. I'm relaxed, comfortable. I don't let my mind wander into worry about my grandfather and what he's probably going to do after he finds out I took his horse. I focus on what I have to do. I'll deal with the rest later.

It takes a while to reach the mountain range. The other horses aren't there and the place is isolated. I don't know where to go from here.

I remember Scout and we head for Skewantee. We land outside the village.

"Sleuchd," I command and Dagda puts his knees to the ground. I wander around looking for someone, anyone. Many of the huts have been destroyed, burnt to the ground. "Scout," I shout in a whisper. "Scout," I say louder this time.

"Who are you?" I voice from behind me asks. I turn around.

"Oh, it is you. The Secret. What are you doing here? You must leave at once. You are not wanted. You have brought much harm to my people. You must go. You must go, now." Scout is insistent. His nose twitches frantically.

"I'm sorry. I don't mean to bring harm to anyone. I'm trying to find Ruis, The Thorn."

"I want you to go. If I tell you where they hide, you will become the sacrifice then we will all be destroyed."

"That won't happen. Please tell me where they are."

He rubs his furry hands together nervously, pacing back and forth with his huge furry paws shuffling the dust around him. "I don't know what to do," he mumbles.

Lilly, Scout's wife, waddles out of the hut. "Hello, my dear. What brings you here again?"

"I need to know where The Thorn is hiding. They've left the caverns. I have to find them. Someone is in danger."

"If you go twenty miles south, beyond the mountain range, there is a pathway leading to nowhere through a doorway of darkness. It is there you will find them."

"What have you done, woman? This will truly be the end of us," Scout shouts as he tramples off into one of the few huts left standing.

"I'm sorry for all you have suffered," I say sincerely.

"I am putting my trust in you to put an end to it," she says.

I fly south with no idea what she meant about a path to nowhere, but I'm hoping it will all make sense when I get there.

As soon as we pass over the snow-capped mountains, a line in the ground appears; a pathway marked in the soil. We descend, landing in a valley nearby, when I see Ruamna, Mugwort and the palomino grazing. I dismount and make my way down the path. Discomforting sounds ring through the trees meeting me in the darkness of the wood. I'm scared, but in control. I keep moving hoping to see something that will make sense as I remember what Lilly told me.

A piece of wood lies in the middle of the trail. As I get closer, I notice a handle on it. I lift the handle as a gush of musty air brushes over me as I open the door in the ground. A ladder leading to a dark abyss invites me into the underworld. There are no lights and I have no idea where I'm headed. With each step of uncertainty I move deeper into the underground.

As I delve deeper into the hole, I hear the echoes of voices flowing from the darkness. The sounds grow louder and turn into the bitter edge of screams. My foot finally meets the last rung and I step onto the ground below me. I head toward a flicker that turns into a brighter light. The sounds of the screamer grow louder and more horrifying with each step. I meander through passageway after passageway, each one giving up very little light, each one holding the secrets of evil.

I turn the corner and see a brighter light moving about. As I get closer to the source of illumination, I see them. Rowen is going to be mad. Surprisingly, I don't care at this point. I'm going to prove myself. I'm going to save my friend, the friend who's lost everything because of me. Ruis captured her in order get to me and he's going to get what he asked for.

I walk up on the three sentries, none of them aware of my presence until they hear my voice. "Have you found her?"

The three of them jump out of their skins, and turn around. Shock and awe. That pretty much explains their expressions.

"How did you get here?" Rowen says loud of enough to resonate.

"The same way you did," I respond.

"Ashe, you shouldn't have come. It's not safe for you." Rowen is surprised and confused.

"I don't need protecting." I may sound a little too sure of myself, but I'm tired of being seen as the damsel in distress.

"What's gotten into you?" Rowen asks.

"She's crazy," Coll adds with abhorrence. Rowen looks at me as if I've lost my mind. I ignore it. I only want to find Taylie.

"Do you know where she is?" I ask Rowen, who's still looking at me as if he's seen a ghost.

"No, but she's got to be down here," Alder jumps in. I follow behind them as we march through the underworld to pursue the echoes.

"That's Taylie," I say as my head begins to pound. We're getting closer, her voice sounds as if it's coming from every direction. The air is thick and hot without any form of ventilation. The dirt walls add to the stench around us.

"Help!" she cries out.

"Here, this way." Alder leads us down another passageway. The darkness swallows us whole. Her voice is clearer but I can tell she's getting weaker by the minute. I want to call out to her to let her know we're coming; to let her know we haven't forgotten her but doing so will put her at more risk.

We turn down another passageway and at the end of it is a room and chained in the corner is Taylie. She's been beaten pretty badly. She's weak and worn. When she sees us, her battered face lights up. Rowen raises his sword and slams the blade over the chains that hold her. As metal hits metal, the chains are broken, but the cuffs remain around her tiny wrist rubbing her skin raw. Coll scoops her up and she wraps her arms around his neck. We sprint out weaving our way through the maze of darkness.

We make our way to the exit. Alder leads the procession up the ladder, as Coll carries Taylie out of the pits of hell, Ruis' hell. Rowen climbs out behind me. We make it back to the horses. Coll and Taylie get on Mugwort and Alder on the palomino. Escape is their only concern. Coll and Alder leave with Taylie on flying horseback.

Rowen pauses when he sees Dagda. "You rode him? You actually made it here on Dagda?"

"I did," I say with pride. I'm tired of being the cause of all the problems. I'm taking responsibility for who and what I am. There's more to me than the helpless bithling everyone believes me to be.

As we're about to embark on our exit, Ruis steps out from behind a tree. He's alone. His head shaven, separating himself from his heritage, his faerie purity, his brethren.

"You're not taking her back, Rowen," Ruis says. His voice is hoarse and lacks the luster that once endowed his words.

Rowen holds up his sword and Ruis joins the invitation. The clash of metal rings throughout the carbon air. They're going at it pretty hard when Rowen falls into a hole that's been covered by twigs and brush. It's a trap. He's at least eight feet under and there's no way out.

"Ashe," he calls as if he's let me down again.

"Looks like it's you and me," Ruis says as he circles me. I follow his every step.

I have no weapon. Only my gift. "We don't have to do this, Ruis, try and remember who you are. Who you once were," I plead for his soul.

"You keep your hands off of her!" Rowen yells from the pit. "Run, Ashe!"

I do the opposite. I'm going to face this. I'm going to deal with this once and for all. No one else is going to die at my expense.

"This is who I am. I was born to lead The Thorn. I was born to be an immortal, as you were born to die." He's almost drooling.

Before I realize it, he raises his sword over me and brings it down over my head. I jump back and catch the blade in its path between the palms of my hands. I hold it steady as my anger transforms the metal into heat. As our gazes meet, I search for a glimpse of purity in the vague twinkle of his eyes. His eyes seethe with the repugnance and the lust for the power that now possesses him. He holds tight to the handle of the sword, tremors vibrating through it. The heat builds up in the weapon as I hold it tightly. I don't know how much longer he'll be able to withstand. His hands shake violently as he loses his grip. He stands unarmed not wanting to touch me, but wanting to kill me.

"This isn't over," he growls and disappears into the darkness that knows him. I drop the sword to the ground as it turns to red ember. The difference between Straif and Ruis, is Ruis knows my capabilities and he isn't going to risk his plans by being over confident.

"Ashe, answer me!" Rowen never stopped calling out.

"He's gone. I'm all right." I peer into the hole keeping him captive.

I grab a vine and throw it in. As Rowen pulls, the dried up vine snaps in two. I try to reach and snatch his hand, but he's too far in down for me to rescue.

"Hold on a second," I say as my mind moves way out of the box for an idea.

I get on Dagda's back and we walk over to the hole. I get off the horse and back him toward the edge of Rowen's trap.

"Take hold of his tail," I instruct. The white flowing tail is so long it easily reaches Rowen.

"Have you totally lost your mind, Ashe?"

"Do it, Rowen. Do you trust me?" I ask as he has asks me many times before.

He grips Dagda's tail with apprehension and I urge the horse forward. With a few steps, Rowen emerges covered in dirt.

I jump off and run back to check on him. He grabs me holding me close. I'm now wearing the dirt that covered him.

"I don't know how this all happened. I don't know how you pulled it off, but it appears I need you more than you need me." Whatever anger, whatever frustration he had is gone.

"Oh, but you're wrong. We need each other," I say. The touch of his caressing hand smudges dirt on my face and around the back of my neck.

28

Acrimony is tense and a sense of confusion saturates the air. Taylie is in bad shape. I run to her bedside.

"Why doesn't Coll do something? What is he waiting for?" For some reason she's throwing up profusely and her color is a shade of green I haven't seen before.

"Coll tried multiple times to heal her, but to no avail. She hasn't responded to anything," Alder tells us.

I watch her sleeping, but it isn't a peaceful sleep. She groans each time she tries to move. Her face is still so swollen. She doesn't look like Taylie.

"Can he heal humans?" I ask.

"Yes, of course. Coll can't heal himself. He should be able to heal her. None of this is making sense." Alder is frustrated with the lack of answers.

Taylie is so weak. What else could happen? She has lost her family, lost her world, her home; everything. Now, she's trying to survive. Her face is battered and there are cuts up and down her arms and legs.

I sit at her bedside wiping her face with cool rags and holding her hand using my gift to calm her. She's begins resting quietly for the first time in hours. Rowen sits across the room waiting with me. Ivy stays, as well, trying to do anything she can to keep Taylie comfortable.

Rowen falls asleep in an arm chair. I think about what we've been through in such a short time and that he's known of me so much longer than I've known of him. Then I look at my best friend so worn and beaten. I want for her what I have. My, how the tables have turned.

Coll shows up. "How is she?" he asks.

"She's resting, finally. She's had a rough night." I pause looking at him as if he's the cause of her pain. "Why can't you heal her?"

"I don't know. I've tried, using every inch of my strength. I don't understand why I can't make her well." He's somber and his eyes fill with fluid as if he's about to cry. He must have something in his eye. I don't believe he can feel, especially for a human.

The morning sun warms the room as it peeks through the window behind Taylie's bed. Coll sleeps in the chair opposite me. My back aches from the wood that's made its mark in my skin during the night. Taylie wakes up. "Where am I?" she mumbles.

"You're safe in Acrimony," I tell her.

She lifts her head, trying to orient herself. "I feel so sick to my stomach," she says.

"Lie down. You need to save your strength. You are going to be all right. Rest." I hope I'm telling her the truth. She reclines back on the pillow and falls quickly back to sleep.

Rowen wakes up and stands behind me with his hand on my shoulder. "Is she any better?"

"She slept all night, but she doesn't look any better and she's still very weak."

Arcos comes in to check on her. Rowen kicks Coll's ankle, startling him.

"What?" Then he sees Arcos standing at the foot of the bed and he's quickly on his feet.

My grandfather is concerned for her. He tells Ivy she is an innocent human who sacrificed to help those of Durt only to meet the evil part of this world. She was thrown in with no knowledge of the faery world and no choice to be a part of it. Actually, it's ironic. Taylie and I were brought here with no choice of our own, with no say.

Wolfsbane comes into the room a few moments later.

"I want Wolfsbane to see if he can tell us what is wrong with her. There is more to her condition than we can see."

We all step away from the bed. Wolfsbane towers over Taylie

while she sleeps. With his eyes closed, he passes his hands over her from head to foot, never touching her. His eyes curl with curiosity until he reaches her abdomen and his forehead wrinkles. His hands pass over her again stopping around her pelvis. When he finishes, he backs away from the bed and drops into the chair behind him. His expression is broken with terror.

"What is it?" Arcos asks.

"My lord, I cannot bear to say it." Wolfsbane's voice is weak to respond.

"What is it? Is she going to survive?" Arco's voice reverberates through the room.

"Worse, my lord."

Coll looks petrified. My heart sinks as Rowen steadies me.

"What do you mean?" I ask.

Wolfsbane hesitates to respond. "She's pregnant."

"She's what?" I ask unsure of what he said.

"With twins. Bithling twins."

The room grows cold and all eyes turn to Coll.

In the luxury of the sitting room, Arcos sits, head bowed, his shoulders quivering. The royal image I have of my grandfather unravels as he carries an enormous weight, and I wonder what it means for all of us.

"Come, Ashe, let's leave him in solitude." Rowen's fingers are in mine and he urges me out of the room.

"But..." I say in protest. "I can't leave him like this."

"What can you say? What can any of us do now?" Rowen tugs at me again. "Taylie needs us. More than ever."

I allow him to pull me away. He's right. Taylie is in for a struggle of unknown proportions. We head for her room, hand-in-hand. One thing is for sure, life in Durt will never be the same.

The End...

Special thanks to:

Royce, I love you! Thanks for always being there for me.

Amy Goggans, Holly Buckingham and
Stephanie Ridley…the best daughters a mom could have. I love you
all very much.

My momma, Itsuko Sheffield, for encouraging me to read.

Janette Porter, you've always been there for me. I don't know what
I would do without you.

Ellen Sallas, a wonderful friend, editor, illustrator and writing
mastermind. You have helped me so much….Isn't this fun?!

Jade Maldonado, you're always there to make sure I don't go too
crazy…too late. I can't believe you've put up with me all these
years.

Lori Simpson, the best PR person in the entire universe.

Deborah Harper and Lynda Strickland, and Beth Lara love you
guys and everyone else who loves to read.

Donna DePriest for support and friendship.

I LOVE YOU ALL SO MUCH!

About the Author

As a child, K F Ridley was labeled as the kid with too much energy. Desperately, she did her best to conform to the ways of the world. Later, to realize she had to be true to herself. As a result, her imagination went wild.

These days, she funnels her energy, exuberance, and high-jinx into *The Dirt Trilogy,* as well as, *The C. Walker Adventures*, beginning with, *The Curse of Yama*. There's no telling where her mind will take her—and you—next.

She lives in Mississippi with her family, her three dogs, two miniature horses (Sunny and Boogie), a miniature donkey (Dobey), and a pot belly pig (Baxter).

Contact the Author:
kfridleybooks@gmail.com
www.kfridley.com
https://www.facebook.com/KFRidleyBooks
Twitter@Kim_Ridley

Join the conversation at #Dirt

Also from Little Roni Publishers

RABBIT: CHASING BETH RIDER by
Ellen C. Maze
**A curiously spiritual vampire tale that is
wowing readers of all ages.**

**Who ever thought writing a best seller could
be so dangerous? Author Beth Rider is**
facing the most terrifying trial of her life against
creatures known only in fables as she
unintentionally threaten the very existence of a
powerful and accursed people. **In the climactic
mêlée, it is a race to the death, or if Beth
has her way, a race to the life-of every
Rakum who makes the choice.**
Fiction / Christian Thriller / Vampire, available in Kindle and Print

THE JUDGING by Ellen C. Maze
**What happens when you want to do the
will of God, but are cursed for all
eternity?**

**Father Marcus Corescu knows.
Transformed into a vampire in 1640
without his knowledge, the young priest
spends his nights "judging" sinners,
simultaneously feeding his newfound
bloodlust.**
Four centuries pass, now posing as a
doctor, Mark no longer recalls his origins. Still
killing, he finds a man who will challenge his
long-held beliefs that he is doing God's will.
**But just because his eyes are opened does not necessarily mean that
his ways are easily changed.**
Fiction / Christian Thriller / Vampire, available in Kindle and Print

Little Roni Publishers
Byhalia, MS
www.littleronipublishers.com

Made in the USA
Charleston, SC
06 February 2014